1 3 5 7 9 10 8 6 4 2

Vintage
20 Vauxhall Bridge Road,
London SW1V 2SA

Vintage Classics is part of the Penguin Random House
group of companies whose addresses can be found at
global.penguinrandomhouse.com.

 Penguin
Random House
UK

*Black Boy* first published in the United Kingdom by Victor Gollancz in 1946
*Native Son* first published in the United Kingdom by Victor Gollancz in 1940
This short edition published by Vintage in 2018

penguin.co.uk/vintage

A CIP catalogue record for this book is available from the British Library

ISBN 9781784874087

Typeset in 9.5/14.5 pt FreightText Pro
by Jouve (UK), Milton Keynes
Printed and bound by Clays Ltd, St Ives plc

Penguin Random House is committed to a sustainable future for
our business, our readers and our planet. This book is made from
Forest Stewardship Council® certified paper.

# Injustice

# RICHARD WRIGHT

**VINTAGE MINIS**

# Black Boy

TO KEEP US out of mischief, my mother often took my brother and me with her to her cooking job. Standing hungrily and silently in a corner of the kitchen, we would watch her go from the stove to the sink, from the cabinet to the table. I always loved to stand in the white folks' kitchen when my mother cooked, for it meant that I got occasional scraps of bread and meat; but many times I regretted having come, for my nostrils would be assailed with the scent of food that did not belong to me and which I was forbidden to eat. Toward evening my mother would take the hot dishes into the dining room where the white people were seated, and I would stand as near the dining-room door as possible to get a quick glimpse of the white faces gathered around the loaded table, eating, laughing, talking. If the white people left anything, my brother and I would eat well; but if they did not, we would have our usual bread and tea.

Watching the white people eat would make my empty

stomach churn and I would grow vaguely angry. Why could I not eat when I was hungry? Why did I always have to wait until others were through? I could not understand why some people had enough food and others did not.

I now found it irresistible to roam during the day while my mother was cooking in the kitchens of the white folks. A block away from our flat was a saloon in front of which I used to loiter all day long. Its interior was an enchanting place that both lured and frightened me. I would beg for pennies, then peer under the swinging doors to watch the men and women drink. When some neighbor would chase me away from the door, I would follow the drunks about the streets, trying to understand their mysterious mumblings, pointing at them, teasing them, laughing at them, imitating them, jeering, mocking, and taunting them about their lurching antics. For me the most amusing spectacle was a drunken woman stumbling and urinating, the dampness seeping down her stockinged legs. Or I would stare in horror at a man retching. Somebody informed my mother about my fondness for the saloon and she beat me, but it did not keep me from peering under the swinging doors and listening to the wild talk of drunks when she was at work.

One summer afternoon – in my sixth year – while peering under the swinging doors of the neighborhood saloon, a black man caught hold of my arm and dragged me into its smoky and noisy depths. The odor of alcohol stung my nostrils. I yelled and struggled, trying to break free of him, afraid of the staring crowd of men and women, but he would not let me go. He lifted me and sat me upon the counter, put his hat upon my head and ordered a drink for me. The tipsy men and women yelled with delight. Somebody tried to jam a cigar into my mouth, but I twisted out of the way.

'How do you feel, setting there like a man, boy?' a man asked.

'Make 'im drunk and he'll stop peeping in here,' somebody said.

'Let's buy 'im drinks,' somebody said.

Some of my fright left as I stared about. Whisky was set before me.

'Drink it, boy,' somebody said.

I shook my head. The man who had dragged me in urged me to drink it, telling me that it would not hurt me. I refused.

'Drink it; it'll make you feel good,' he said.

I took a sip and coughed. The men and women laughed. The entire crowd in the saloon gathered about me now, urging me to drink. I took another sip. Then another. My head spun and I laughed. I was put on the floor and I ran giggling and shouting among the yelling crowd. As I would pass each man, I would take a sip from an offered glass. Soon I was drunk.

A man called me to him and whispered some words into my ear and told me that he would give me a nickel if I went to a woman and repeated them to her. I told him that I would say them; he gave me the nickel and I ran to the woman and shouted the words. A gale of laughter went up in the saloon.

'Don't teach that boy that,' someone said.

'He doesn't know what it is,' another said.

From then on, for a penny or a nickel, I would repeat to anyone whatever was whispered to me. In my foggy, tipsy state the reaction of the men and women to my mysterious words enthralled me. I ran from person to person, laughing, hiccoughing, spewing out filth that made them bend double with glee.

'Let that boy alone now,' someone said.

'It ain't going to hurt 'im,' another said.

'It's a shame,' a woman said, giggling.

'Go home, boy,' somebody yelled at me.

Toward early evening they let me go. I staggered along the pavements, drunk, repeating obscenities to the horror of the women I passed and to the amusement of the men en route to their homes from work.

To beg drinks in the saloon became an obsession. Many evenings my mother would find me wandering in a daze and take me home and beat me; but the next morning, no sooner had she gone to her job than I would run to the saloon and wait for someone to take me in and buy me a drink. My mother protested tearfully to the proprietor of the saloon, who ordered me to keep out of his place. But the men – reluctant to surrender their sport – would buy me drinks anyway, letting me drink out of their flasks on the streets, urging me to repeat obscenities.

I was a drunkard in my sixth year, before I had begun school. With a gang of children, I roamed the streets, begging pennies from passers-by, haunting the doors of saloons, wandering farther and farther away from home each day. I saw more than I could understand and heard more than I could remember. The point of life became for me the times when I could beg drinks. My mother was in despair. She beat me; then she prayed and wept over me, imploring me to be good, telling me that she had to work, all of which carried no weight to my wayward mind. Finally she placed me and my brother in the keeping of an old black woman who watched me every moment to keep me from running to the doors of the saloons to beg for whisky. The craving for alcohol finally left me and I forgot the taste of it.

*

WE WERE AT the railroad station with our bags, waiting for the train that would take us to Arkansas; and for the first time I noticed that there were two lines of people at the ticket window, a 'white' line and a 'black' line. During my visit at Granny's a sense of the two races had been born in me with a sharp concreteness that would never die until I died. When I boarded the train I was aware that we Negroes were in one part of the train and that the whites were in another. Naively I wanted to go and see how the whites looked while sitting in their part of the train.

'Can I go and peep at the white folks?' I asked my mother.

'You keep quiet,' she said.

'But that wouldn't be wrong, would it?'

'Will you keep still?'

'But why can't I?'

'Quit talking foolishness!'

I had begun to notice that my mother became irritated when I questioned her about whites and blacks, and I could not quite understand it. I wanted to understand these two sets of people who lived side by side and never touched, it seemed, except in violence. Now, there was my grandmother . . . Was she white? Just how white was she? What did the whites think of her whiteness?

'Mama, is Granny white?' I asked as the train rolled through the darkness.

'If you've got eyes, you can see what color she is,' my mother said.

'I mean, do the white folks think she's white?'

'Why don't you ask the white folks that?' she countered.

'But you know,' I insisted.

'Why should I know?' she asked. 'I'm not white.'

'Granny looks white,' I said, hoping to establish one fact, at least. 'Then why is she living with us colored folks?'

'Don't you want Granny to live with us?' she asked, blunting my question.

'Yes.'

'Then why are you asking?'

I wanted to understand these two sets of people who lived side by side and never touched, it seemed, except in violence

'I want to *know*.'

'Doesn't Granny live with us?'

'Yes.'

'Isn't that enough?'

'But does she *want* to live with us?'

'Why didn't you ask Granny that?' my mother evaded me again in a taunting voice.

'Did Granny become colored when she married Grandpa?'

'Will you stop asking silly questions!'

'But did she?'

'Granny didn't *become* colored,' my mother said angrily. 'She was *born* the color she is now.'

Again I was being shut out of the secret, the thing, the reality I felt somewhere beneath all the words and silences.

'Why didn't Granny marry a white man?' I asked.

'Because she didn't want to,' my mother said peevishly.

'Why don't you want to talk to me?' I asked.

She slapped me and I cried. Later, grudgingly, she told me that Granny came of Irish, Scotch, and French stock in which Negro blood had somewhere and somehow been infused. She explained it all in a matter-of-fact, offhand, neutral way; her emotions were not involved at all.

'What was Granny's name before she married Grandpa?'

'Bolden.'

'Who gave her that name?'

'The white man who owned her.'

'She was a slave?'

'Yes.'

'And Bolden was the name of Granny's father?'

'Granny doesn't know who her father was.'

'So they just gave her any name?'

'They gave her a name; that's all I know.'

'Couldn't Granny find out who her father was?'

'For what, silly?'

'So she could know.'

'Know for what?'

'Just to know.'

'But for *what*?'

I could not say. I could not get anywhere.

'Mama, where did Father get his name?'

'From his father.'

'And where did the father of my father get his name?'

'Like Granny got hers. From a white man.'

'Do they know who he is?'

'I don't know.'

'Why don't they find out?'

'For what?' my mother demanded harshly.

And I could think of no rational or practical reason why my father should try to find out who his father's father was.

'What has Papa got in him?' I asked.

'Some white and some red and some black,' she said.

'Indian, white, and Negro?'

'Yes.'

'Then what am I?'

'They'll call you a colored man when you grow up,' she said. Then she turned to me and smiled mockingly and asked: 'Do you mind, Mr. Wright?'

I was angry and I did not answer. I did not object to being called colored, but I knew that there was something my mother was holding back. She was not concealing facts, but feelings, attitudes, convictions which she did not want me to know; and she became angry when I prodded her. All right, I would find out someday. Just wait. All right, I was colored. It was fine. I did not know enough to be afraid or to anticipate in a concrete manner. True, I had heard that colored people were killed and beaten, but so far it all had seemed remote. There was, of course, a vague uneasiness about it all, but I would be able to handle that when I came to it. It would be simple. If anybody tried to kill me, then I would kill them first.

# Fear

BIGGER CUPPED HIS hand to his mouth and spoke through an imaginary telephone transmitter.

'Hello.'

'Hello,' Gus answered. 'Who's this?'

'This is the President of the United States speaking,' Bigger said.

'Oh, yessuh, Mr President,' Gus said.

'I'm calling a cabinet meeting this afternoon at four o'clock and you, as Secretary of State, *must* be there.'

'Well, now, Mr President,' Gus said, 'I'm pretty busy. They raising sand over there in Germany and I got to send 'em a note . . .'

'But this is important,' Bigger said.

'What you going to take up at this cabinet meeting?' Gus asked.

'Well, you see, the niggers is raising sand all over the country,' Bigger said, struggling to keep back his laughter. 'We've got to do something with these black folks . . .'

'Oh, if it's about the niggers, I'll be right there, Mr President,' Gus said.

They hung up imaginary receivers and leaned against the wall and laughed. A streetcar rattled by, Bigger sighed and swore.

'Goddammit!'

'What's the matter?'

'They don't let us do *nothing*.'

'Who?'

'The *white* folks.'

'You talk like you just now finding that out,' Gus said.

'Naw. But I just can't get used to it,' Bigger said. 'I swear to God I can't. I know I oughtn't think about it, but I can't help it. Every time I think about it I feel like somebody's poking a red-hot iron down my throat. Goddammit, look! We live here and they live there. We black and they white. They got things and we ain't. They do things and we can't. It's just like living in jail. Half the time I feel like I'm on the outside of the world peeping in through a knot-hole in the fence . . .'

'Aw, ain't no use feeling that way about it. It don't help none,' Gus said.

'You know one thing?' Bigger said.

'What?'

'Sometimes I feel like something awful's going to happen to me,' Bigger spoke with a tinge of bitter pride in his voice.

'What you mean?' Gus asked, looking at him quickly. There was fear in Gus's eyes.

'I don't know. I just feel that way. Every time I get to thinking about me being black and they being white, me being here and they being there, I feel like something awful's going to happen to me . . .'

'Aw, for chrissakes! There ain't nothing you can do about it. How come you want to worry yourself? You black and they make the laws . . .'

'Why they make us live in one corner of the city? Why don't they let us fly planes and run ships . . .'

Gus hunched Bigger with his elbow and mumbled good-naturedly, 'Aw, nigger, quit thinking about it. You'll go nuts.'

Because he was restless and had time on his hands, Bigger yawned again and hoisted his arms high above his head.

'Nothing ever happens,' he complained.

'What you want to happen?'

'Anything,' Bigger said with a wide sweep of his dingy palm, a sweep that included all the possible activities of the world.

Then their eyes were riveted; a slate-colored pigeon swooped down to the middle of the steel car tracks and began strutting to and fro with ruffled feathers, its fat neck bobbing with regal pride. A streetcar rumbled forward and the pigeon rose swiftly through the air on wings stretched so taut and sheer that Bigger could see the gold of the sun through their translucent tips. He tilted his head and watched the slate-colored bird flap and wheel out of sight over the edge of a high roof.

'Now, if I could only do that,' Bigger said.

Gus laughed.

'Nigger, you nuts.'

'I reckon we the only things in this city that can't go where we want to go and do what we want to do.'

'Don't think about it,' Gus said.

'I can't help it.'

'That's why you feeling like something awful's going to happen to you,' Gus said. 'You think too much.'

'What in hell can a man do?' Bigger asked, turning to Gus.

'Get drunk and sleep it off.'

'I can't. I'm broke.'

Bigger crushed his cigarette and took out another one and offered the package to Gus. They continued smoking. A huge truck swept past, lifting scraps of white paper into the sunshine; the bits settled down slowly.

'Gus?'

'Hunh?'

'You how where the white folks live?'

'Yeah,' Gus said, pointing eastward. 'Over across the "line"; over there on Cottage Grove Avenue.'

'Naw; they don't,' Bigger said.

'What you mean?' Gus asked, puzzled. 'Then, where do they live?'

Bigger doubled his fist and struck his solar plexus.

'Right down here in my stomach,' he said.

Gus looked at Bigger searchingly, then away, as though ashamed.

'Yeah; I know what you mean,' he whispered.

'Every time I think of 'em, I *feel* 'em,' Bigger said.

'Yeah; and in your chest and throat, too,' Gus said.

'It's like fire.'

'And sometimes you can't hardly breathe . . .'

Bigger's eyes were wide and placid, gazing into space.

'That's when I feel like something awful's going to happen to me . . .' Bigger paused, narrowed his eyes. 'Naw; it ain't like something going to happen to me. It's . . . It's like I was going to do something I can't help . . .'

'Yeah!' Gus said with uneasy eagerness. His eyes were full of a look compounded of fear and admiration for Bigger. 'Yeah; I know what you mean. It's like you going to fall and don't know where you going to land . . .'

Gus's voice trailed off. The sun slid behind a big white cloud and the street was plunged in cool shadow; quickly the sun edged forth again and it was bright and warm once more. A long sleek black car, its fenders glinting like glass in the sun, shot past them at high speed and turned a corner a few blocks away. Bigger pursed his lips and sang:

'Zooooooooooom!'

'They got everything,' Gus said.

'They own the world,' Bigger said.

# How 'Bigger' was born

THE BIRTH OF Bigger Thomas goes back to my childhood, and there was not just one Bigger, but many of them, more than I could count and more than you suspect. But let me start with the first Bigger, whom I shall call Bigger No. 1.

When I was a bareheaded, barefoot kid in Jackson, Mississippi, there was a boy who terrorized me and all of the boys I played with. If we were playing games, he would saunter up and snatch from us our balls, bats, spinning tops, and marbles. We would stand around pouting, sniffling, trying to keep back our tears, begging for our playthings. But Bigger would refuse. We never demanded that he give them back; we were afraid, and Bigger was bad. We had seen him clout boys when he was angry and we did not want to run that risk. We never recovered our toys unless we flattered him and made him feel that he was superior to us. Then, perhaps, if he felt like it, he condescended, threw them at us and then gave each of us a swift kick in the bargain, just to make us feel his utter contempt.

That was the way Bigger No. 1 lived. His life was a continuous challenge to others. At all times he *took* his way, right or wrong, and those who contradicted him had him to fight. And never was he happier than when he had someone cornered and at his mercy; it seemed that the deepest meaning of his squalid life was in him at such times.

I don't know what the fate of Bigger No. 1 was. His swaggering personality is swallowed up somewhere in the amnesia of my childhood. But I suspect that his end was violent. Anyway, he left a marked impression upon me; maybe it was because I longed secretly to be like him and was afraid. I don't know.

If I had known only one Bigger I would not have written *Native Son*. Let me call the next one Bigger No. 2; he was about seventeen and tougher than the first Bigger. Since I, too, had grown older, I was a little less afraid of him. And the hardness of this Bigger No. 2 was not directed toward me or the other Negroes, but toward the whites who ruled the South. He bought clothes and food on credit and would not pay for them. He lived in the dingy shacks of the white landlords and refused to pay rent. Of course, he had no money, but neither did we. We did without the necessities of life and starved ourselves, but he never would. When we asked him why he acted as he did, he would tell us (as though we were little children in a kindergarten) that the white folks had everything and he had nothing. Further, he would tell us that we were fools not to get what we wanted while we were alive in this world. We would listen and silently agree. We longed to believe and act as he did, but we were afraid. We were Southern Negroes and we were hungry and we wanted to live, but we were more willing to tighten our belts than risk conflict. Bigger No. 2 wanted to live and he did; he was in prison the last time I heard from him.

There was Bigger No. 3, whom the white folks called a 'bad nigger'. He carried his life in his hands in a literal fashion. I once worked as a ticket-taker in a Negro movie house (all movie houses in Dixie are Jim Crow; there are movies for whites and movies for blacks), and many times Bigger No. 3 came to the door and gave my arm a hard pinch and walked into the theater. Resentfully and silently, I'd nurse my bruised arm. Presently, the proprietor would come over and ask how things were going. I'd point into the darkened theater and say: 'Bigger's in there.' 'Did he pay?' the proprietor would ask. 'No, sir,' I'd answer. The proprietor would pull down the corners of his lips and speak through his teeth: 'We'll kill that goddamn nigger one of these days.' And the episode would end right there. But later on Bigger No. 3 was killed during the days of Prohibition: while delivering liquor to a customer he was shot through the back by a white cop.

And then there was Bigger No. 4, whose only law was death. The Jim Crow laws of the South were not for him. But as he laughed and cursed and broke them, he knew that some day he'd have to pay for his freedom. His rebellious spirit made him violate all the taboos and consequently he always oscillated between moods of intense elation and depression. He was never happier than when he had outwitted some foolish custom, and he was never more melancholy than when brooding over the impossibility of his ever being free. He had no job, for he regarded digging ditches for fifty cents a day as slavery. 'I can't live on that', he would say. Ofttimes I'd find him reading a book; he would stop and in a joking, wistful, and cynical manner ape the antics of the white folks. Generally, he'd end his mimicry in a depressed state and say: 'The white folks won't let us do nothing.' Bigger No. 4 was sent to the asylum for the insane.

Then there was Bigger No. 5, who always rode the Jim Crow streetcars without paying and sat wherever he pleased. I remember one morning his getting into a streetcar (all streetcars in Dixie are divided into two sections: one section is for whites and is labeled – FOR WHITES; the other section is for Negroes and is labeled – FOR COLORED) and sitting in the white section. The conductor went to him and said: 'Come on, nigger. Move over where you belong. Can't you read?' Bigger answered: 'Naw, I can't read.' The conductor flared up: 'Get out of that seat!' Bigger took out his knife, opened it, held it nonchalantly in his hand and replied: 'Make me.' The conductor turned red, blinked, clenched his fists, and walked away, stammering: 'The goddamn scum of the earth!' A small angry conference of white men took place in the front of the car and the Negroes sitting in the Jim Crow section overheard: 'That's that Bigger Thomas nigger and you'd better leave 'im alone.' The Negroes experienced an intense flash of pride and the streetcar moved on its journey without incident. I don't know what happened to Bigger No. 5. But I can guess.

The Bigger Thomases were the only Negroes I know of who consistently violated the Jim Crow laws of the South and got away with it, at least for a sweet brief spell. Eventually, the whites who restricted their lives made them pay a terrible price. They were shot, hanged, maimed, lynched, and generally hounded until they were either dead or their spirits broken.

There were many variations to this behavioristic pattern. Later on I encountered other Bigger Thomases who did not react to the locked-in Black Belts with the same extremity and violence. But before I use Bigger Thomas as a springboard for the examination of milder types, I'd better indicate more precisely the nature of the environment that produced these men, or the reader will be left with the impression that they were essentially and organically bad.

In Dixie there are two worlds, the white world and the black world, and they are physically separated. There are white schools and black schools, white churches and black churches, white businesses and black businesses, white graveyards and black graveyards, and, for all I know, a white God and a black God . . .

This separation was accomplished after the Civil War by the terror of the Ku Klux Klan, which swept the newly freed Negro through arson, pillage, and death out of the United States Senate, the House of Representatives, the many state legislatures, and out of the public, social, and economic life of the South. The motive for this assault was simple and urgent. The imperialistic tug of history had torn the Negro from his African home and had placed him ironically upon the most fertile plantation areas of the South; and, when the Negro was freed, he outnumbered the whites in many of these fertile areas.

Hence, a fierce and bitter struggle took place to keep the ballot from the Negro, for had he had a chance to vote, he would have automatically controlled the richest lands of the South and with them the social, political, and economic destiny of a third of the Republic. Though the South is politically a part of America, the problem that faced her was peculiar and the struggle between the whites and the blacks after the Civil War was in essence a struggle for power, ranging over thirteen states and involving the lives of tens of millions of people.

But keeping the ballot from the Negro was not enough to hold him in check; disfranchisement had to be supplemented by a whole panoply of rules, taboos, and penalties designed not only to insure peace (complete submission) but to guarantee that no real threat would ever arise. Had the Negro lived upon a common territory, separate from the bulk of the white population, this program of oppression might not have assumed such a brutal and violent form. But this war took place between people who were neighbors, whose homes adjoined, whose farms had common boundaries. Guns and disfranchisement, therefore, were not enough to make the black neighbor keep his distance. The white neighbor decided to limit the amount of education his black neighbor could receive; decided to keep him off the police force and out of the local national guards; to segregate him residentially; to Jim Crow him in public places; to restrict his participation in the professions and jobs; and to build up a vast, dense ideology of racial superiority that would justify any act of violence taken against him to defend white dominance; and further, to condition him to hope for little and to receive that little without rebelling.

But, because the blacks were so *close* to the very civilization which sought to keep them out, because they could not *help* but react in some way to its incentives and prizes, and because the very tissue of their consciousness received its tone and timbre from the strivings of that dominant civilization, oppression spawned among them a myriad variety of reactions, reaching from outright blind rebellion to a sweet, other-worldly submissiveness.

In the main, this delicately balanced state of affairs has not greatly altered since the Civil War, save in those parts of the South which have been industrialized or urbanized. So volatile and tense are these relations that if a Negro rebels against rule and taboo, he is lynched and the reason for the lynching is usually called 'rape', that catchword which has garnered such vile connotations that it can raise a mob anywhere in the South pretty quickly, even today.

FOR A LONG time I toyed with the idea of writing a novel in which a Negro Bigger Thomas would loom as a symbolic figure of American life, a figure who would hold within him the prophecy of our future. I felt strongly that he held within him, in a measure which perhaps no other contemporary type did, the outlines of action and feeling which we would encounter on a vast scale and in the days to come. Just as one sees when one walks into a medical research laboratory jars of alcohol containing abnormally large or distorted portions of the human body, just so did I see and feel that the conditions of life under which Negroes are forced to live in America contain the embryonic emotional prefigurations of how a large part of the body politic would react under stress.

So, with this much knowledge of myself and the world gained and known, why should I not try to work out on paper the problem of what will happen to Bigger? Why should I not, like a scientist in a laboratory, use my imagination and invent test-tube situations, place Bigger in them, and, following the guidance of my own hopes and fears, what I had learned and remembered, work out in fictional form an emotional statement and resolution of this problem?

But several things militated against my starting to work. Like Bigger himself, I felt a mental censor – product of the fears which a Negro feels from living in America – standing over me, draped in white, warning me not to write. This censor's warnings were translated into my own thought processes thus: 'What will white people think if I draw the picture of such a Negro boy? Will they not at once say: "See, didn't we tell you all along that nig-gers are like that? Now, look, one of their own kind has come along and drawn the picture for us!"' I felt that if I drew the picture of Bigger truthfully, there would be many reactionary whites who would try to make of him something I did not intend. And yet, and this was what made it difficult, I knew that I could not write of Bigger convincingly if I did not depict him as he *was*: that is, resentful toward whites, sullen, angry, ignorant, emotion-ally unstable, depressed and unaccountably elated at times, and unstable even, because of his own lack of inner organization which American oppression has fostered in him, to unite with the members of his own race. And would not whites misread Bigger and, doubting his authenticity, say: 'This man is preaching hate against the whole white race'?

The more I thought of it the more I became convinced that if I did not write of Bigger as I saw and felt him, if I did not try to make him a living personality and at the same time a symbol of all the larger things I felt and saw in him, I'd be reacting as Bigger himself reacted: that is,

I'd be acting out of *fear* if I let what I thought whites would say constrict and paralyze me.

As I contemplated Bigger and what he meant, I said to myself: 'I must write this novel, not only for others to read, but to free *myself* of this sense of shame and fear.' In fact, the novel, as time passed, grew upon me to the extent that it became a necessity to write it; the writing of it turned into a way of living for me.

Another thought kept me from writing. What would my own white and black comrades in the Communist party say? This thought was the most bewildering of all. Politics is a hard and narrow game; its policies represent the aggregate desires and aspirations of millions of people. Its goals are rigid and simply drawn, and the minds of the majority of politicians are set, congealed in terms of daily tactical maneuvers. How could I create such complex and wide schemes of associational thought and feeling, such filigreed webs of dreams and politics, without being mistaken for a 'smuggler of reaction', 'an ideological confusionist', or 'an individualistic and dangerous element'? Though my heart is with the collectivist and proletarian ideal, I solved this problem by assuring myself that honest politics and honest feeling in imaginative representation ought to be able to meet on common healthy ground without fear, suspicion, and quarreling. Further, and more importantly, I steeled myself by coming to the conclusion that whether politicians accepted or rejected Bigger did not really matter; my task, as I felt it, was to free myself of this burden of impressions and feelings, recast them into the image of Bigger and make him *true*. Lastly, I felt that a right more immediately deeper than that of politics or race was at stake; that is, a *human* right, the right of a man to think and feel honestly. And especially did this personal and human right bear hard upon me, for temperamentally I am inclined to satisfy the claims of my own ideals rather than the expectations of others. It was this obscure need that had pulled me into the labor movement in the beginning and by exercising it I was but fulfilling what I felt to be the laws of my own growth.

There was another constricting thought that kept me from work. It deals with my own race. I asked myself: 'What will Negro doctors, lawyers, dentists, bankers, school teachers, social workers and business men, think of me if I draw such a picture of Bigger?' I knew from long and painful experience that the Negro middle and professional classes were the people of my own race who were more than others ashamed of Bigger and what he meant. Having narrowly escaped the Bigger Thomas reaction pattern themselves – indeed, still retaining traces of it within the confines of their own timid personalities – they would not relish being publicly reminded of the lowly, shameful depths of life above which they enjoyed their bourgeois lives. Never did they want people, especially *white* people, to think that their lives were so much touched by anything so dark and brutal as Bigger.

Their attitude toward life and art can be summed up in a single paragraph: 'But, Mr Wright, there are so many of us who are *not* like Bigger. Why don't you portray in your fiction the *best* traits of our race, something that will show the white people what we have done in *spite* of oppression? Don't represent anger and bitterness. Smile when a white person comes to you. Never let him feel that you are so small that what he had done to crush you has made you hate him! Oh, above all, save your *pride*!'

But Bigger won over all these claims; he won because I felt that I was hunting on the trail of more exciting and thrilling game. What Bigger meant had claimed me because I felt with all of my being that he was more important than what any person, white or black, would say or try to make of him, more important than any political analysis designed to explain or deny him, more important, even, than my own sense of fear, shame, and diffidence.

# Flight

WITHOUT ITS MAKING a clear picture in his mind, he understood how it had happened. Some of the bones had not burnt and had fallen into the lower bin when he had worked the handle to sift the ashes. The white man had poked in the shovel to clear the air passage and had raked them out. And now there they lay, tiny, oblong pieces of white bone, cushioned in gray ashes. He could not stay here now. At any moment they would begin to suspect him. They would hold him; they would not let him go even if they were not certain whether he had done it or not. And Jan was still in jail, swearing that he had an alibi. They would know that Mary was dead; they had stumbled upon the white bones of her body. They would be looking for the murderer. The men were silent, bent over, poking into the pile of gray ashes. Bigger saw the hatchet blade come into view. God! The whole world was tumbling down. Quickly, Bigger's eyes looked at their bent backs; they were not watching him. The red glare of the fire lit their faces and the draft of the furnace drummed. Yes; he would go, now! He tiptoed to the rear of the furnace and stopped, listening. The men were whispering in tense tones of horror.

'It's the girl!'

'Good God!'

'Who do you suppose did it?'

Bigger tiptoed up the steps, one at a time, hoping that the roar of the furnace and the men's voices and the scraping of the shovel would drown out the creaking sounds his feet made. He reached the top of the steps and breathed deeply, his lungs aching from holding themselves full of air so long. He stole to the door of his room and opened it and went in and pulled on the light. He turned to the window and put his hands under the upper ledge and lifted; he felt a cold rush of air laden with snow. He heard muffled shouts downstairs and the inside of his stomach glowed white-hot. He ran to the door and locked it and then turned out the light. He groped, to the window and climbed into it, feeling again the chilling blast of snowy wind. With his feet upon the bottom ledge, his legs bent under him, his sweaty body shaken by wind, he looked into the snow and tried to see the ground below; but he could not. Then he leaped, headlong, sensing his body twisting in the icy air as he hurtled. His eyes were shut and his hands were clenched as his body turned, sailing through the snow. He was in the air a moment; then he hit. It seemed at first that he hit softly, but the shock of it went through him, up his back to his head and he lay buried in a cold pile of snow, dazed. Snow was in his mouth, eyes, ears; snow was seeping down his back. His hands were wet and cold. Then he felt all of the muscles of his body contract violently, caught in a spasm of reflex action, and at the same time he felt his groin laved with warm water. It was his urine. He had not been able to control the muscles of his hot body against the chilled assault of the wet snow over all his skin. He lifted his head, blinking his eyes, and looked above him. He sneezed. He was himself now; he struggled against the snow, pushing it away from him. He got to his feet, one at a time, and pulled himself out. He walked, then tried to run; but he felt too weak. He went down Drexel Boulevard, not knowing just where he was heading, but knowing that he had to get out of this white neighborhood. He avoided the car line, turned down dark streets, walking more rapidly now, his eyes before him, but turning now and then to look behind.

Yes, he would have to tell Bessie not to go to that house. It was all over. He had to save himself. But it was familiar, this running away. All his life he had been knowing that sooner or later something like this would come to him. And now, here it was. He had always felt outside of this white world, and now it was true. It made things simple. He felt in his shirt. Yes; the gun was still there. He might have to use it. He would shoot before he would let them take him; it meant death either way, and he would die shooting every slug he had.

He came to Cottage Grove Avenue and walked southward. He could not make any plans until he got to Bessie's and got the money. He tried to shut out of his mind the fear of being caught. He lowered his head against the driving snow and tramped through the icy streets with clenched fists. Although his hands were almost frozen, he did not want to put them in his pockets, for that would have made him feel that he would not have been ready to defend himself were the police to accost him suddenly. He went on past street lamps covered with thick coatings of snow, gleaming like huge frosted moons above his head. His face ached from the sub-zero cold and the wind cut into his wet body like a long sharp knife going to the heart of him with pain.

He was in sight of Forty-seventh Street now. He saw, through a gauzelike curtain of snow, a boy standing under an awning selling papers. He pulled his cap visor lower and slipped into a doorway to wait for a car. Back of the newsboy was a stack of papers piled high upon a newsstand. He wanted to see the tall black headline, but the driving snow would not let him. The papers ought to be full of him now. It did not seem strange that they should be, for all his life he had felt that things had been happening to him that should have gone into them. But only after he had acted upon feelings which he had had for years would the papers carry the story, *his* story. He felt that they had not wanted to print it as long as it had remained buried and burning in his own heart. But now that he had thrown it out, thrown it at those who made him live as they wanted, the papers were printing it. He fished two cents out of his pocket; he went over to the boy with averted face.

'Tribune.'

He took the paper into a doorway. His eyes swept the streets above the top of it; then he read in tall black type: MILLIONAIRE HEIRESS KIDNAPPED. ABDUCTORS DEMAND $10,000 IN RANDOM NOTE. DALTON FAMILY ASK RELEASE OF COMMUNIST SUSPECT. Yes; they had it now. Soon they would have the story of her death, of the reporters' finding her bones in the furnace, of her head being cut off, of his running away during the excitement. He looked up, hearing the approach of a car. When it heaved into sight he saw it was almost empty of passengers. Good! He ran into the street and reached the steps just as the last man got on. He paid his fare, watching to see if the conductor was noticing him; then went through the car, watching to see if any face was turned to him. He stood on the front platform, back of the motorman. If anything happened he could get off quickly here. The car started and he opened the paper again, reading:

A servant's discovery early yesterday evening of a crudely penciled ransom note demanding $10,000 for the return of Mary Dalton, missing Chicago heiress, and the Dalton family's sudden demand for the release of Jan Erlone,

Communist leader held in connection with the girl's dis-
appearance, were the startling developments in a case
which is baffling local and state police.

The note, bearing the signature of 'Red' and the famed
hammer and sickle emblem of the Communist Party, was
found sticking under the front door by Peggy O'Flagherty,
a cook and housekeeper in the Henry Dalton residence in
Hyde Park.

Bigger read a long stretch of type in which was
described the 'questioning of a Negro chauffeur', 'the
half-packed trunk', 'the Communist pamphlets', 'drunken
sexual orgies', 'the frantic parents', and 'the radical's con-
tradictory story'. Bigger's eyes skimmed the words:
'clandestine meetings offered opportunities for abduc-
tion', 'police asked not to interfere in case', 'anxious
family trying to contact kidnappers'; and:

It was conjectured that perhaps the family had informa-
tion to the effect that Erlone knew of the whereabouts of
Miss Dalton, and certain police officials assigned that as
the motive behind the family's request for the radical's
release.

Reiterating that police had framed him as part of a
drive to oust Communists from Chicago, Erlone
demanded that the charges upon which he had been origi-
nally held be made public. Failing to obtain a satisfactory
answer, he refused to leave jail, whereupon police again

remanded him to his cell upon a charge of disorderly
conduct.

Bigger lifted his eyes and looked about; no one was watching him. His hand was shaking with excitement. The car
moved lumberingly through the snow and he saw that he
was near Fiftieth Street. He stepped to the door and said,
'Out.'

The car stopped and he swung off into the driving
snow. He was almost in front of Bessie's now. He looked
up to her window; it was dark. The thought that she might
not be in her room, but out drinking with friends, made
him angry. He went into the vestibule. A dim light glowed
and his body was thankful for the meager warmth. He
could finish reading the paper now. He unfolded it; then,
for the first time, he saw his picture. It was down in the
lower left-hand corner of page two. Above it he read:
REDS TRIED TO SNARE HIM. It was a small picture
and his name was under it; he looked solemn and black
and his eyes gazed straight and the white cat sat perched
upon his right shoulder, its big round black eyes twin
pools of secret guilt. And, oh! Here was a picture of Mr
and Mrs Dalton standing upon the basement steps. That
the image of Mr and Mrs Dalton which he had seen but
two hours ago should be seen again so soon made him
feel that this whole vague white world which could do
things this quickly was more than a match for him, that
soon it would track him down and have it out with him.

The white-haired old man and the white-haired old woman standing on the steps with their arms stretched forth pleading were a powerful symbol of helpless suffering and would stir up a lot of hate against him when it was found out that a Negro had killed Mary.

Bigger's lips tightened. There was no chance of his getting that money now. They had found Mary and would stop at nothing to get the one who had killed her. There would be a thousand white policemen on the South Side searching for him or any black man who looked like him.

He pressed the bell and waited for the buzzer to ring. Was she there? Again he pressed the bell, holding his finger hard upon it until the door buzzed. He bounded up the steps, sucking his breath in sharply at each lift of his knees. When he reached the second landing he was breathing so hard that he stopped, closed his eyes and let his chest heave itself to stillness. He glanced up and saw Bessie staring sleepily at him through the half-opened door. He went in and stood for a moment in the darkness.

'Turn on the light,' he said.

'Bigger! What's happened?'

'Turn on the light!'

She said nothing and did not move. He groped forward, sweeping the air with his open palm for the cord; he found it and jerked on the light. Then he whirled and looked about him, expecting to see someone lurking in the corners of the room.

'What's happened?' she came forward and touched his clothes. 'You're wet.'

'It's all off,' he said.

'I don't have to do it?' she asked eagerly.

Yes; she was thinking only of herself now. He was alone.

'Bigger, tell me what happened?'

'They know all about it. They'll be after me soon.'

Her eyes were too filled with fear to cry. He walked about aimlessly and his shoes left rings of dirty water on the wooden floor.

'Tell me, Bigger! Please!'

She was wanting the word that would free her of this nightmare; but he would not give it to her. No; let her be with him; let somebody be with him now. She caught hold of his coat and he felt her body trembling.

'Will they come for me, too, Bigger? I didn't want to do it!'

Yes, he would let her know, let her know everything; but let her know it in a way that would bind her to him, at least a little longer. He did not want to be alone now.

'They found the girl,' he said.

'What we going to do, Bigger? Look what you done to me . . .'

She began to cry.

'Aw, come on, kid.'

'You *really* killed her?'

'She's dead,' he said. 'They found her.'

She ran to the bed, fell upon it and sobbed. With her mouth all twisted and her eyes wet, she asked in gasps:

'Y-y-you d-didn't send the l-letter?'

'Yeah.'

'Bigger,' she whimpered.

'There ain't no help for it now.'

'Oh, Lord! They'll come for me. They'll know you did it and they'll go to your home and talk to your ma and brother and everybody. They'll come for me now sure.'

That was true. There was no way for her but to come with him. If she stayed here they would come to her and she would simply lie on the bed and sob out everything. She would not be able to help it. And what she would tell them about him, his habits, his life, would help them to track him down.

'You got the money?'

'It's in my dress pocket.'

'How much is it?'

'Ninety dollars.'

'Well, what you planning to do?' he asked.

'I wish I could kill myself.'

'Ain't no use talking that way.'

'There ain't no way else to talk.'

It was a shot in the dark, but he decided to try it.

'If you don't act better'n this, I'll just leave.'

'Naw; naw ... Bigger!' she cried, rising and running to him.

'Well, snap out of it,' he said, backing to a chair. He sat

down and felt how tired he was. Some strength he did not know he possessed had enabled him to run away, to stand here and talk with her; but now he felt that he would not have strength enough to run even if the police should suddenly burst into the room.

'You h-hurt?' she asked, catching hold of his shoulder.

He leaned forward in the chair and rested his face in the palms of his hands.

'Bigger, what's the matter?'

'I'm tired and awful sleepy,' he sighed.

'Let me fix you something to eat.'

'I need a drink.'

'Naw; no whiskey. You need some hot milk.'

He waited, hearing her move about. It seemed that his body had turned to a piece of lead that was cold and heavy and wet and aching. Bessie switched on her electric stove, emptied a bottle of milk into a pan and set it upon the glowing red circle. She came back to him and placed her hands upon his shoulders, her eyes wet with fresh tears.

'I'm scared, Bigger.'

'You can't be scared now.'

'You oughtn't've killed her, honey.'

'I didn't mean to, I couldn't help it. I swear!'

'What happened? You never told me.'

'Aw, hell. I was in her room . . .'

'*Her* room?'

'Yeah. She was drunk. She passed out. I . . . I took her there.'

'What she do?'

'She . . . Nothing. She didn't do anything. Her ma came in. She's blind . . .'

'The girl?'

'Naw; her ma. I didn't want her to find me there. Well, the girl was trying to say something and I was scared. I just put the edge of the pillow in her mouth and . . . I didn't mean to kill her. I just pulled the pillow over her face and she died. Her ma came into the room and the girl was trying to say something and her ma had her hands stretched out, like this, see? I was scared she was going to touch me. I just sort of pushed the pillow hard over the girl's face to keep her from yelling. Her ma didn't touch me; I got out of the way. But when she left I went to the bed and the girl . . . She . . . She was dead . . . That was all. She was dead . . . I didn't mean . . .'

'You didn't plan to kill her?'

'Naw; I swear I didn't. But what's the use? Nobody'll believe me.'

'Honey. Don't you see?'

'What?'

'They'll say . . .'

Bessie cried again. He caught her face in his hands. He was concerned; he wanted to see this thing through her eyes at that moment.

'What?'

'They'll . . . They'll say you raped her.'

Bigger stared. He had entirely forgotten the moment

when he had carried Mary up the stairs. So deeply had he pushed it all back down into him that it was not until now that its real meaning came back. They would say he had raped her and there would be no way to prove that he had not. That fact had not assumed importance in his eyes until now. He stood up, his jaws hardening. Had he raped her? Yes, he had raped her. Every time he felt as he had felt that night, he raped. But rape was not what one did to women. Rape was what one felt when one's back was against a wall and one had to strike out, whether one wanted to or not, to keep the pack from killing one. He committed rape every time he looked into a white face. He was a long, taut piece of rubber which a thousand white hands had stretched to the snapping point, and when he snapped it was rape. But it was rape when he cried out in hate deep in his heart as he felt the strain of living day by day. That, too, was rape.

\*

'HEY!'

As he ducked down the alley he saw the man standing in the snow looking at him and he knew that the man would not follow.

'Hey, you!'

He scrambled to the window, pitched the paper in before him, caught hold and heaved himself upward onto

**He was a long, taut piece of rubber which a thousand white hands had stretched to the snapping point**

the ledge and then inside. He landed on his feet and stood peering through the window into the alley; all was white and quiet. He picked up the paper and walked down the hallway to the steps and up to the third floor, using the flashlight and hearing his footsteps echo faintly in the empty building. He stopped, clutched his pocket in panic as his mouth flew open. Yes; he had it. He thought that he had dropped the gun when he had fallen in the snow, but it was still there. He sat on the top step of the stairs and opened out the paper, but for quite awhile he did not read. He listened to the creaking of the building caused by the wind sweeping over the city. Yes; he was alone; he looked down and read, REPORTERS FIND DALTON GIRL'S BONES IN FURNACE. NEGRO CHAUFFEUR DIS-APPEARS. FIVE THOUSAND POLICE SURROUND BLACK BELT. AUTHORITIES HINT SEX CRIME. COMMUNIST LEADER PROVES ALIBI. GIRL'S MOTHER IN COLLAPSE. He paused and reread the line, AUTHORITIES HINT SEX CRIME. Those words excluded him utterly from the world. To hint that he had committed a sex crime was to pronounce the death sentence; it meant a wiping out of his life even before he was captured; it meant death before death came, for the white men who read those words would at once kill him in their hearts.

The Mary Dalton kidnapping case was dramatically cracked wide open when a group of local newspaper reporters accidentally discovered several bones, later positively established as those of the missing heiress, in the furnace of the Dalton home late today . . .

Search of the Negro's home, 3721 Indiana Avenue, in the heart of the South Side, failed to reveal his whereabouts. Police expressed belief that Miss Dalton met her death at the hands of the Negro, perhaps in a sex crime, and that the white girl's body was burned to destroy evidence.

Bigger looked up. His right hand twitched. He wanted a gun in that hand. He got his gun from his pocket and held it. He read again:

Immediately a cordon of five thousand police, augmented by more than three thousand volunteers, was thrown about the Black Belt. Chief of Police Glenman said this morning that he believed that the Negro was still in the city, since all roads leading in and out of Chicago were blocked by a record-breaking snowfall.

Indignation rose to white heat last night as the news of the Negro's rape and murder of the missing heiress spread through the city.

Police reported that many windows in the Negro sections were smashed.

Every street car, bus, el train and auto leaving the South Side is being stopped and searched. Police and vigilantes, armed with rifles, tear gas, flashlights, and photos of the killer, began at 18th Street this morning and are searching every Negro home under a blanket warrant from the mayor. They are making a careful search of all abandoned buildings, which are said to be hideouts for Negro criminals.

Maintaining that they feared for the lives of their children, a delegation of white parents called upon Superintendent of City Schools Horace Minton, and begged that all schools be closed until the Negro rapist and murderer was captured.

Reports were current that several Negro men were beaten in various North and West Side neighborhoods.

In the Hyde Park and Englewood districts, men organized vigilante groups and sent word to Chief of Police Glenman offering aid.

Glenman said this morning that the aid of such groups would be accepted. He stated that a woefully undermanned police force together with recurring waves of Negro crime made such a procedure necessary.

Several hundred Negroes resembling Bigger Thomas were rounded up from South Side 'hot spots'; they are being held for investigation.

In a radio broadcast last night Mayor Ditz warned of possible mob violence and exhorted the public to maintain order. 'Every effort is being made to apprehend this fiend,' he said.

It was reported that several hundred Negro employees

throughout the city had been dismissed from jobs. A well-known banker's wife phoned this paper that she had dismissed her Negro cook, 'for fear that she might poison the children.'

Bigger's eyes were wide and his lips were parted; he scanned the print quickly: 'handwriting experts busy', 'Erlone's fingerprints not found in Dalton home', 'radical still in custody'; and then a sentence leaped at Bigger, like a blow:

Police are not yet satisfied with the account Erlone has given of himself and are of the conviction that he may be linked to the Negro as an accomplice; they feel that the plan of the murder and kidnapping was too elaborate to be the work of a Negro mind.

At that moment he wanted to walk out into the street and up to a policeman and say, 'No! Jan didn't help me! He didn't have a damn thing to do with it! I – I did it!' His lips twisted in a smile that was half-leer and half-defiance.

Holding the paper in taut fingers, he read phrases: 'Negro ordered to clean out ashes ... reluctant to respond ... dreading discovery . . . smoke-filled basement . . . tragedy of communism and racial mixture . . . possibility that kidnap note was work of reds . . .'

Bigger looked up. The building was quiet save for the continual creaking caused by the wind. He could not stay here. There was no telling when they were coming into this neighborhood. He could not leave Chicago; all roads were blocked, and all trains, buses and autos were being stopped and searched. It would have been much better if he had tried to leave town at once. He should have gone to some other place, perhaps Gary, Indiana, or Evanston. He looked at the paper and saw a black-and-white map of the South Side, around the borders of which was a shaded portion an inch deep. Under the map ran a line of small print:

Shaded portion shows area already covered by police and vigilantes in search for Negro rapist and murderer. White portion shows area yet to be searched.

\*

HE PASSED A bakery and wanted to go in and buy some rolls with the seven cents he had. But the bakery was empty of customers and he was afraid that the white proprietor would recognize him. He would wait until he came to a Negro business establishment, but he knew that there were not many of them. Almost all businesses in the Black Belt were owned by Jews, Italians, and Greeks. Most Negro businesses were funeral parlors; white undertakers refused to bother with dead black bodies. He came to a chain grocery store. Bread sold here for five cents a loaf, but across the 'line' where white folks lived, it sold for four. And now, of all times, he could not cross that 'line'. He stood looking through the plate glass at the people inside. Ought he to go in? He had to. He was starving. They trick us every breath we draw! he thought. They gouge our eyes out! He opened the door and walked to the counter. The warm air made him dizzy; he caught hold of a counter in front of him and steadied himself. His eyes blurred and there swam before him a vast array of red and blue and green and yellow cans stacked high upon shelves. All about him he heard the soft voices of men and women.

'You waited on, sir?'

'A loaf of bread,' he whispered.

'Anything else, sir?'

'Naw.'

The man's face went away and came again; he heard paper rustling.

'Cold out, isn't it?'

'Hunh? Oh, yessuh.'

He laid the nickel on the counter; he saw the blurred loaf being handed to him.

'Thank you. Call again.'

He walked unsteadily to the door with the loaf under his arm. Oh, Lord! If only he could get into the street! In the doorway he met people coming in; he stood to one side to let them pass, then went into the cold wind, looking for an empty flat. At any moment he expected to hear his name shouted; expected to feel his arms being grabbed. He walked five blocks before he saw a two-story flat building with a 'For Rent' sign in a window. Smoke bulged out of chimneys and he knew that it was warm inside. He went to the front door and read the little vacancy notice pasted on the glass and saw that the flat was a rear one. He went down the alley to the rear steps and mounted to the second floor. He tried a window and it slid up easily. He was in luck. He hoisted himself through and dropped into a warm room, a kitchen. He was suddenly tense, listening. He heard voices, they seemed to be coming from the room in front of him. Had he made a mistake? No. The kitchen was not furnished; no one, it seemed, lived in here. He tiptoed to the next room and found it empty; but he heard the voices even more clearly now. He saw still another room leading farther; he tiptoed and looked. That room, too, was empty, but the sound of the voices was coming so loud that he could make out the words. An argument was going on in the front flat. He stood with the loaf of bread in his hands, his legs wide apart, listening.

'Jack, yuh mean t' stan' there 'n' say yuh'd give tha' nigger up t' the white folks?'

'Damn right Ah would!'

'But, Jack, s'pose he ain' guilty?'

'Whut in hell he run off fer then?'

'Mabbe he thought they wuz gonna blame the murder on *him*!'

'Lissen, Jim. Ef he wuzn't guilty, then he oughta stayed 'n' faced it. Ef Ah knowed where tha' nigger wuz Ah'd turn 'im up 'n' git these white folks off me.'

'But, Jack, *ever*' nigger looks guilty t' white folks when somebody's done a crime.'

'Yeah; tha's 'cause so many of us ack like Bigger Thomas; tha's all. When yuh ack like Bigger Thomas yuh stir up trouble.'

'But, Jack, who's stirring up trouble now? The papers say they beatin' us up all over the city. They don' care whut black man they git. We's all dogs in they sight! Yuh gotta stan' up 'n' fight these folks.'

''N' git killed? Hell, naw! Ah gotta family. Ah gotta wife 'n' baby. Ah ain't startin' no fool fight. Yuh can't git no justice pertectin' men who kill . . .'

'We's *all* murderers t' them, Ah tell yuh!'

'Lissen, Jim. Ah'm a hard-workin' man. Ah fixes the streets wid a pick an' shovel ever' day, when Ah git a chance. But the boss tol' me he didn't wan' me in them streets wid this mob feelin' among the white folks . . . He says Ah'll git killed. So he lays me off. Yuh see, tha' god-damn nigger Bigger Thomas made me lose mah job . . . He made the white folks think we's *all* jus' like him!'

'But, Jack, Ah tell yuh they think it awready. Yuh's a good man, but tha' ain' gonna keep 'em from comin' t' yo' home, is it? Hell, naw! We's all black 'n' we jus' as waal *ack* black, don' yuh see?'

'Aw, Jim, it's awright t' git mad, but yuh gotta look at things straight. Tha' guy made me lose mah job. Tha' ain' fair! How is Ah gonna eat? Ef Ah knowed where the black sonofabitch wuz Ah'd call the cops 'n' let 'em come 'n' git 'im!'

'Waal, Ah wouldn't. Ah'd die firs'!'

'Man, yuh crazy! Don' yuh wan' a home 'n' wife 'n' chil-lun? Whut's fightin' gonna git yuh? There's *mo'* of them than us. They could kill us all. Yuh gotto learn t' live 'n' git erlong wid people.'

'When folks hate me, Ah don' wanna git erlong.'

'But we gotta *eat*! We gotta *live*!'

'Ah don' care! Ah'd die firs'!'

'Aw, hell! Yuh crazy!'

'Ah don' care whut yuh say. Ah'd die 'fo' Ah'd let 'em scare me inter tellin' on tha' man. Ah tell yuh, Ah'd die firs'!'

# Fate

THERE WAS NO day for him now, and there was no night; there was but a long stretch of time, a long stretch of time that was very short; and then – the end. Toward no one in the world did he feel any fear now, for he knew that fear was useless; and toward no one in the world did he feel any hate now, for he knew that hate would not help him.

Though they carried him from one police station to another, though they threatened him, persuaded him, bullied him, and stormed at him, he steadfastly refused to speak. Most of the time he sat with bowed head, staring at the floor; or he lay full length upon his stomach, his face buried in the crook of an elbow, just as he lay now upon a cot with the pale yellow sunshine of a February sky falling obliquely upon him through the cold steel bars of the Eleventh Street Police Station.

Food was brought to him upon trays and an hour later the trays were taken away, untouched. They gave him packages of cigarettes, but they lay on the floor, unopened.

He would not even drink water. He simply lay or sat, saying nothing, not noticing when anyone entered or left his cell. When they wanted him to go from one place to another, they caught him by the wrist and led him; he went without resistance, walking always with dragging feet, head down. Even when they snatched him up by the collar, his weak body easily lending itself to be manhandled, he looked without hope or resentment, his eyes like two still pools of black ink in his flaccid face. No one had seen him save the officials and he had asked to see no one. Not once during the three days following his capture had an image of what he had done come into his mind. He had thrust the whole thing back of him, and there it lay, monstrous and horrible. He was not so much in a stupor, as in the grip of a deep physiological resolution not to react to anything.

Having been thrown by an accidental murder into a position where he had sensed a possible order and meaning in his relations with the people about him; having accepted the moral guilt and responsibility for that murder because it had made him feel free for the first time in his life; having felt in his heart some obscure need to be at home with people and having demanded ransom money to enable him to do it – having done all this and failed, he chose not to struggle any more. With a supreme act of will springing from the essence of his being, he turned away from his life and the long train of disastrous consequences that had flowed from it and looked wistfully upon the dark face of ancient waters upon which some spirit had breathed and created him, the dark face of the waters from which he had been first made in the image of a man with a man's obscure need and urge; feeling that he wanted to sink back into those waters and rest eternally.

And yet his desire to crush all faith in him was in itself built upon a sense of faith. The feelings of his body reasoned that if there could be no merging with the men and women about him, there should be a merging with some other part of the natural world in which he lived. Out of the mood of renunciation there sprang up in him again the will to kill. But this time it was not directed outward toward people, but inward, upon himself. Why not kill that wayward yearning within him that had led him to this end? He had reached out and killed and had not solved anything, so why not reach inward and kill that which had duped him? This feeling sprang up of itself, organically, automatically; like the rotted hull of a seed forming the soil in which it should grow again.

And, under and above it all, there was the fear of death before which he was naked and without defense; he had to go forward and meet his end like any other living thing upon the earth. And regulating his attitude toward death was the fact that he was black, unequal, and despised. Passively, he hungered for another orbit between two poles that would let him live again; for a new mode of life that would catch him up with the tension of hate and love. There would have to hover above him, like the stars in a full sky, a vast configuration of images and symbols whose magic and power could lift him up and make him live so intensely that the dread of being black and unequal would be forgotten; that even death would not matter, that it would be a victory. This would have to happen before he could look them in the face again: a new pride and a new humility would have to be born in him, a humility springing from a new identification with some part of the world in which he lived, and this identification forming the basis for a new hope that would function in him as pride and dignity.

But maybe it would never come; maybe there was no such thing for him; maybe he would have to go to his end just as he was, dumb, driven, with the shadow of emptiness in his eyes. Maybe this was all. Maybe the confused promptings, the excitement, the tingling, the elation – maybe they were false lights that led nowhere. Maybe they were right when they said that a black skin was bad, the covering of an apelike animal. Maybe he was just unlucky, a man born for dark doom, an obscene joke happening amid a colossal din of siren screams and white faces and circling lances of light under a cold and silken sky. But he could not feel that for long; just as soon as his feelings reached such a conclusion, the conviction that there was some way out surged back into him, strong and powerful, and, in his present state, condemning and paralyzing.

And then one morning a group of men came and caught

**Maybe he was just unlucky, a man born for dark doom, an obscene joke happening amid a colossal din of siren screams**

him by the wrists and led him into a large room in the Cook County Morgue, in which there were many people. He blinked from the bright lights and heard loud and excited talking. The compact array of white faces and the constant flashing of bulbs for pictures made him stare in mounting amazement. His defense of indifference could protect him no longer. At first he thought that it was the trial that had begun, and he was prepared to sink back into his dream of nothingness. But it was not a court room. It was too informal for that. He felt crossing his feelings a sensation akin to the same one he had had when the reporters had first come into Mr Dalton's basement with their hats on, smoking cigars and cigarettes, asking questions; only now it was much stronger. There was in the air a silent mockery that challenged him. It was not their hate he felt; it was something deeper than that. He sensed that in their attitude toward him they had gone beyond hate. He heard in the sound of their voices a patient certainty; he saw their eyes gazing at him with calm conviction. Though he could not have put it into words, he felt that not only had they resolved to put him to death, but that they were determined to make his death mean more than a mere punishment; that they regarded him as a figment of that black world which they feared and were anxious to keep under control. The atmosphere of the crowd told him that they were going to use his death as a bloody symbol of fear to wave before the eyes of that black world. And as he felt it, rebellion rose in him. He had sunk to the lowest point this side of death, but when he felt his life again threatened in a way that meant that he was to go down the dark road a helpless spectacle of sport for others, he sprang back into action, alive, contending.

He tried to move his hands and found that they were shackled by strong bands of cold steel to white wrists of policemen sitting to either side of him. He looked round; a policeman stood in front of him and one in back. He heard a sharp, metallic click and his hands were free. There was a rising murmur of voices and he sensed that it was caused by his movements. Then his eyes became riveted on a white face, tilted slightly upward. The skin had a quality of taut anxiety and around the oval of white face was a framework of whiter hair. It was Mrs Dalton, sitting quietly, her frail, waxen hands folded in her lap. Bigger remembered as he looked at her that moment of stark terror when he had stood at the side of the bed in the dark blue room hearing his heart pound against his ribs with his fingers upon the pillow pressing down upon Mary's face to keep her from mumbling.

Sitting beside Mrs Dalton was Mr Dalton, looking straight before him with wide-open, unblinking eyes. Mr Dalton turned slowly and looked at Bigger and Bigger's eyes fell.

He saw Jan: blond hair; blue eyes; a sturdy, kind face looking squarely into his own. Hot shame flooded him as the scene in the car came back; he felt again the pressure of Jan's fingers upon his hand. And then shame was replaced by guilty anger as he recalled Jan's confronting him upon the sidewalk in the snow.

He was getting tired; the more he came to himself, the more a sense of fatigue seeped into him. He looked down at his clothes; they were damp and crumpled and the sleeves of his coat were drawn halfway up his arms. His shirt was open and he could see the black skin of his chest. Suddenly, he felt the fingers of his right hand throb with pain. Two fingernails were torn off. He could not remember how it had happened. He tried to move his tongue and found it swollen. His lips were dry and cracked and he wanted water. He felt giddy. The lights and faces whirled slowly, like a merry-go-round. He was falling swiftly through space . . .

When he opened his eyes he was stretched out upon a cot. A white face loomed above him. He tried to lift his body and was pushed back.

'Take it easy, boy. Here; drink this.'

A glass touched his lips. Ought he to drink? But what difference did it make? He swallowed something warm; it was milk. When the glass was empty he lay upon his back and stared at the white ceiling; the memory of Bessie and the milk she had warmed for him came back strongly. Then the image of her death came and he closed his eyes, trying to forget. His stomach growled; he was feeling better. He heard a low drone of voices. He gripped the edge of the cot and sat up.

'Hey! How're you feeling, boy?'

'Hunh?' he grunted. It was the first time he had spoken since they had caught him.

'How're you feeling?'

He closed his eyes and turned his head away, sensing that they were white and he was black, that they were the captors and he the captive.

'He's coming out of it.'

'Yeah. That crowd must've got 'im.'

'Say, boy! You want something to eat?'

He did not answer.

'Get 'im something. He doesn't know what he wants.'

'You better lie down, boy. You'll have to go back to the inquest this afternoon.'

He felt their hands pushing him back onto the cot. The door closed; he looked round. He was alone. The room was quiet. He had come out into the world again. He had not tried to; it had just happened. He was being turned here and there by a surge of strange forces he could not understand. It was not to save his life that he had come out; he did not care what they did to him. They could place him in the electric chair right now, for all he cared. It was to save his pride that he had come. He did not want them to make sport of him. If they had killed him that night when they were dragging him down the steps, that would have been a deed born of their strength over him. But he felt they had no right to sit and watch him, to use him for whatever they wanted.

The door opened and a policeman brought in a tray of

food, set it on a chair next to him, and left. There was steak and fried potatoes and coffee. Gingerly, he cut a piece of steak and put it into his mouth. It tasted so good that he tried to swallow it before he chewed it. He sat on the edge of the cot and drew the chair forward so that he could reach the food. He ate so fast that his jaws ached. He stopped and held the food in his mouth, feeling the juices of his glands flowing round it. When he was through, he lit a cigarette, stretched out upon the cot and closed his eyes. He dozed off to an uneasy sleep.

Then suddenly he sat upright. He had not seen a newspaper in a long time. What were they saying now? He got up; he swayed and the room lurched. He was still weak and giddy. He leaned against the wall and walked slowly to the door. Cautiously, he turned the knob. The door swung in and he looked into the face of a policeman.

'What's the matter, boy?'

He saw a heavy gun sagging at the man's hip. The policeman caught him by the wrist and led him back to the cot.

'Here; take it easy.'

'I want a paper,' he said.

'Hunh? A paper?'

'I want to read the paper.'

'Wait a minute. I'll see.'

The policeman went out and presently returned with an armful of papers.

'Here you are, boy. You're in 'em all.'

He did not turn to the papers until after the man had left the room. Then he spread out the *Tribune* and saw: NEGRO RAPIST FAINTS AT INQUEST. He understood now; it was the inquest he had been taken to. He had fainted and they had brought him here. He read:

Overwhelmed by the sight of his accusers, Bigger Thomas, Negro sex-slayer, fainted dramatically this morning at the inquest of Mary Dalton, millionaire Chicago heiress.

Emerging from a stupor for the first time since his capture last Monday night, the black killer sat cowed and fearful as hundreds sought to get a glimpse of him.

'He looks exactly like an ape!' exclaimed a terrified young white girl who watched the black slayer being loaded onto a stretcher after he had fainted.

Though the Negro killer's body does not seem compactly built, he gives the impression of possessing abnormal physical strength. He is about five feet, nine inches tall and his skin is exceedingly black. His lower jaw protrudes obnoxiously, reminding one of a jungle beast.

His arms are long, hanging in a dangling fashion to his knees. It is easy to imagine how this man, in the grip of a brain-numbing sex passion, overpowered little Mary Dalton, raped her, murdered her, beheaded her, then stuffed her body into a roaring furnace to destroy the evidence of his crime.

His shoulders are huge, muscular, and he keeps them hunched, as if about to spring upon you at any moment.

He looks at the world with a strange, sullen, fixed-from-under stare, as though defying all efforts of compassion.

All in all, he seems a beast utterly untouched by the softening influences of modern civilization. In speech and manner he lacks the charm of the average, harmless, genial, grinning southern darky so beloved by the American people.

The moment the killer made his appearance at the inquest, there were shouts of 'Lynch 'im! Kill 'im!'

But the brutish Negro seemed indifferent to his fate, as though inquests, trials, and even the looming certainty of the electric chair held no terror for him. He acted like an earlier missing link in the human species. He seemed out of place in a white man's civilization.

An Irish police captain remarked with deep conviction: 'I'm convinced that death is the only cure for the likes of him.'

For three days the Negro has refused all nourishment. Police believe that he is either trying to starve himself to death and cheat the chair, or that he is trying to excite sympathy for himself.

From Jackson, Mississippi, came a report yesterday from Edward Robertson, editor of the *Jackson Daily Star*, regarding Bigger Thomas' boyhood there. The editor wired:

'Thomas comes of a poor darky family of a shiftless and immoral variety. He was raised here and is known to local residents as an irreformable sneak thief and liar. We were unable to send him to the chain gang because of his extreme youth.

'Our experience here in Dixie with such depraved types of Negroes has shown that only the death penalty, inflicted in a public and dramatic manner, has any influence upon their peculiar mentality. Had that nigger Thomas lived in Mississippi and committed such a crime, no power under Heaven could have saved him from death at the hands of indignant citizens.

'I think it but proper to inform you that in many quarters it is believed that Thomas, despite his dead-black complexion, may have a minor portion of white blood in his veins, a mixture which generally makes for a criminal and intractable nature.

'Down here in Dixie we keep Negroes firmly in their places and we make them know that if they so much as touch a white woman, good or bad, they cannot live.

'When Negroes become resentful over imagined wrongs, nothing brings them to their senses so quickly as when citizens take the law into their hands and make an example out of a trouble-making nigger.

'Crimes such as the Bigger Thomas murders could be lessened by segregating all Negroes in parks, playgrounds, cafés, theatres, and street cars. Residential segregation is imperative. Such measures tend to keep them as much as possible out of direct contact with white women and lessen their attacks against them.

'We of the South believe that the North encourages

Negroes to get more education than they are organically capable of absorbing, with the result that northern Negroes are generally more unhappy and restless than those of the South. If separate schools were maintained, it would be fairly easy to limit the Negroes' education by regulating the appropriation of moneys through city, county, and state legislative bodies.

'Still another psychological deterrent can be attained by conditioning Negroes so that they have to pay deference to the white person with whom they come in contact. This is done by regulating their speech and actions. We have found that the injection of an element of constant fear has aided us greatly in handling the problem.'

He lowered the paper; he could not read any more. Yes, of course; they were going to kill him; but they were having this sport with him before they did it. He held very still; he was trying to make a decision; not thinking, but feeling it out. Ought he to go back behind his wall? *Could* he go back now? He felt that he could not. But would not any effort he made not turn out like the others? Why go forward and meet more hate? He lay on the cot, feeling as he had felt that night when his fingers had gripped the icy edges of the water tank under the roving flares of light, knowing that men crouched below him with guns and tear gas, hearing the screams of sirens and shouts rising thirstily from ten thousand throats . . .

Overcome with drowsiness, he closed his eyes; then opened them abruptly. The door swung in and he saw a black face. Who was this? A tall, well-dressed black man came forward and paused. Bigger pulled up and leaned on his elbow. The man came all the way to the cot and stretched forth a dingy palm, touching Bigger's hand.

'Mah po' boy! May the good Lawd have mercy on yuh.'

He stared at the man's jet-black suit and remembered who he was: Reverend Hammond, the pastor of his mother's church. And at once he was on guard against the man. He shut his heart and tried to stifle all feeling in him. He feared that the preacher would make him feel remorseful. He wanted to tell him to go; but so closely associated in his mind was the man with his mother and what she stood for that he could not speak.

In his feelings he could not tell the difference between what this man evoked in him and what he had read in the papers; the love of his own kind and the hate of others made him feel equally guilty now.

'How yuh feel, son?' the man asked; he did not answer and the man's voice hurried on: 'Yo' ma ast me t' come 'n' see yuh. She wants t' come too.'

The preacher knelt upon the concrete floor and closed his eyes. Bigger clamped his teeth and flexed his muscles; he knew what was coming.

'Lawd Jesus, turn Yo' eyes 'n' look inter the heart of this po' sinner! Yuh said mercy wuz awways Yo's 'n' ef we ast fer it on bended knee Yuh'd po' it out inter our hearts 'n' make our cups run over! We's astin' Yuh t' po' out Yo' mercy now, Lawd! Po' it out fer this po' sinner boy who stan's in deep need of it! Ef his sins be as scarlet, Lawd, wash 'em white as snow! Fergive 'im fer whutever he's done, Lawd! Let the light of Yo' love guide 'im th'u these dark days! 'N' he'p them who's atryin' to he'p 'im, Lawd! Enter inter they hearts 'n' breathe compassion on they sperits! We ast this in the nama Yo' Son Jesus who died on the cross 'n' gave us the mercy of Yo' love! Ahmen . . .'

Bigger stared unblinkingly at the white wall before him as the preacher's words registered themselves in his consciousness. He knew without listening what they meant; it was the old voice of his mother telling of suffering, of hope, of love beyond this world. And he loathed it because it made him feel as condemned and guilty as the voice of those who hated him.

'Son . . .'

Bigger glanced at the preacher, and then away.

'Fergit ever'thing but yo' soul, son. Take yo' mind off ever' thing but eternal life. Fergit whut the newspaper say. Fergit yuh's black. Gawd looks past yo' skin 'n' inter yo' soul, son. He's lookin' at the only parta yuh that's *His*. He wants yuh 'n' He loves yuh. Give yo'se'f t' 'Im, son. Lissen, lemme tell yeh why yuh's here; lemme tell yuh a story tha'll make yo' heart glad . . .'

\*

HE GLANCED UP, hearing the doorknob turn. The door opened and Jan stood framed in it, hesitating. Bigger sprang to his feet, galvanized by fear. The preacher also stood, took a step backward, bowed, and said,

'Good mawnin', suh.'

Bigger wondered what Jan could want of him now. Was he not caught and ready for trial? Would not Jan get his revenge? Bigger stiffened as Jan walked to the middle of the floor and stood facing him. Then it suddenly occurred to Bigger that he need not be standing, that he had no reason to fear bodily harm from Jan here in jail. He sat and bowed his head; the room was quiet, so quiet that Bigger heard the preacher and Jan breathing. The white man upon whom he had tried to blame his crime stood before him and he sat waiting to hear angry words. Well, why didn't he speak? He lifted his eyes; Jan was looking straight at him and he looked away. But Jan's face was not angry. If he were not angry, then what did he want? He looked again and saw Jan's lips move to speak, but no words came. And when Jan did speak his voice was low and there were long pauses between the words; it seemed to Bigger that he was listening to a man talk to himself.

'Bigger, maybe I haven't the words to say what I want to say, but I'm going to try ... This thing hit me like a bomb. It t-t-took me all week to get myself together. They had me in jail and I couldn't for the life of me figure out what was happening ... I – I don't want to worry you, Bigger. I know you're in trouble. But there's something I just got to say ... You needn't talk to me unless you want to, Bigger. I think I know something of what you're feeling now. I'm not dumb, Bigger; I can understand, even if I didn't seem to understand that night ...' Jan paused, swallowed, and lit a cigarette. 'Well, you jarred me ... I see now. I was kind of blind. I – I just wanted to come here and tell you that I'm not angry ... I'm not angry and I want you to let me help you. I don't hate you for trying to blame this thing on me ... Maybe you had good reasons ... I don't know. And maybe in a certain sense, I'm the one who's really guilty ...' Jan paused again and sucked long and hard at his cigarette, blew the smoke out slowly and nervously bit his lips. 'Bigger, I've never done anything against you and your people in my life. But I'm a white man and it would be asking too much to ask you not to hate me, when every white man you see hates you. I – I know my ... my face looks like theirs to you, even though I don't feel like they do. But I didn't know we were so far apart until that night ... I can understand now why you pulled that gun on me when I waited outside that house to talk to you. It was the only thing you could have done; but I didn't know my white face was making you feel guilty, condemning you ...' Jan's lips hung open, but no words came from them; his eyes searched the corners of the room.

Bigger sat silently, bewildered, feeling that he was on a vast blind wheel being turned by stray gusts of wind. The preacher came forward.

'Is yuh Mistah Erlone?'

'Yes,' said Jan, turning.

'Tha' wuz a mighty fine thing you jus' said, suh. Ef any-body needs he'p, this po' boy sho does. Ah'm Reveren' Hammon'.'

Bigger saw Jan and the preacher shake hands.

'Though this thing hurt me, I got something out of it,' Jan said, sitting down and turning to Bigger. 'It made me see deeper into men. It made me see things I knew, but had forgotten. I – I lost something, but I got something, too . . .' Jan tugged at his tie and the room was silent, wait-ing for him to speak. 'It taught me that it's your right to hate me, Bigger. I see now that you couldn't do anything else but that; it was all you had. But, Bigger, if I say you got the right to hate me, then that ought to make things a lit-tle different, oughtn't it? Ever since I got out of jail I've been thinking this thing over and I felt that I'm the one who ought to be in jail for murder instead of you. But that can't be, Bigger. I can't take upon myself the blame for what one hundred million people have done.' Jan leaned forward and stared at the floor. 'I'm not trying to make up to you, Bigger. I didn't come here to feel sorry for you. I don't suppose you're so much worse off than the rest of us who get tangled up in this world. I'm here because I'm trying to live up to this thing as I see it. And it isn't easy, Bigger. I – I loved that girl you killed. I – I loved . . .' His voice broke and Bigger saw his lips tremble. 'I was in jail grieving for Mary and then I thought of all the black men who've been killed, the black men who had to grieve when their people were snatched from them in slavery and since slavery. I thought that if they could stand it, then I ought to.' Jan crushed the cigarette with his shoe. 'At first, I thought old man Dalton was trying to frame me, and I wanted to kill him. And when I heard that you'd done it, I wanted to kill you. And then I got to thinking. I saw if I killed, this thing would go on and on and never stop. I said, "I'm going to help that guy, if he lets me."'

'May Gawd in heaven bless yuh, son,' the preacher said.

Jan lit another cigarette and offered one to Bigger; but Bigger refused by keeping his hands folded in front of him and staring stonily at the floor. Jan's words were strange; he had never heard such talk before. The meaning of what Jan had said was so new that he could not react to it; he simply sat, staring, wondering, afraid even to look at Jan.

'Let me be on your side, Bigger,' Jan said. 'I can fight this thing with you, just like you've started it. I can come from all of those white people and stand here with you. Listen, I got a friend, a lawyer. His name is Max. He understands this thing and wants to help you. Won't you talk to him?'

Bigger understood that Jan was not holding him guilty for what he had done. Was this a trap? He looked at Jan and saw a white face, but an honest face. This white man believed in him, and the moment he felt that belief he felt guilty again; but in a different sense now. Suddenly, this white man had come up to him, flung aside the curtain and walked into the room of his life. Jan had spoken a declaration of friendship that would make other white men hate him: a particle of white rock had detached itself from that looming mountain of white hate and had rolled down the slope, stopping still at his feet. The word had become flesh. For the first time in his life a white man became a human being to him; and the reality of Jan's humanity came in a stab of remorse: he had killed what this man loved and had hurt him. He saw Jan as though someone had performed an operation upon his eyes, or as though someone had snatched a deforming mask from Jan's face.

Bigger started nervously; the preacher's hand came to his shoulder.

'Ah don't wanna break in 'n' meddle where Ah ain' got no bisness, suh,' the preacher said in a tone that was militant, but deferring. 'But there ain' no usa draggin' no communism in this thing, Mistah. Ah respecks yo' feelin's powerfully, suh; but whut yuh's astin' jus' stirs up mo' hate. Whut this po' boy needs is understandin' . . .'

'But he's got to fight for it,' Jan said.

'Ah'm wid yuh when yuh wanna change men's hearts,' the preacher said. 'But Ah can't go wid yuh when yuh wanna stir up mo' hate . . .'

Bigger sat looking from one to the other, bewildered.

'How on earth are you going to change men's hearts when the newspapers are fanning hate into them every day?' Jan asked.

'Gawd kin change 'em!' the preacher said fervently.

Jan turned to Bigger.

'Won't you let my friend help you, Bigger?'

Bigger's eyes looked round the room, as if seeking a means of escape. What could he say? He was guilty.

'Forget me,' he mumbled.

'I can't,' Jan said.

'It's over for me,' Bigger said.

'Don't you believe in yourself?'

'Naw,' Bigger whispered tensely.

'You believed enough to kill. You thought you were settling something, or you wouldn't've killed,' Jan said.

Bigger stared and did not answer. Did this man believe in him *that* much?

'I want you to talk to Max,' Jan said.

Jan went to the door. A policeman opened it from the outside. Bigger sat, open-mouthed, trying to feel where all this was bearing him. He saw a man's head come into the door, a head strange and white, with silver hair and a lean white face that he had never seen before.

'Come on in,' Jan said.

'Thanks.'

The voice was quiet, firm, but kind; there was about the man's thin lips a faint smile that seemed to have always been there. The man stepped inside; he was tall.

'How are you, Bigger?'

Bigger did not answer. He was doubtful again. Was this a trap of some kind?

'This is Reverend Hammond, Max,' Jan said.

Max shook hands with the preacher, then turned to Bigger.

'I want to talk with you,' Max said. 'I'm from the Labor Defenders. I want to help you.'

\*

FOR THE FIRST time since his capture, Bigger felt that he wanted someone near him, something physical to cling to. He was glad when he heard the lock in his door click. He sat up; a guard loomed over him.

'Come on, boy. Your lawyer's here.'

He was handcuffed and led down the hall to a small room where Max stood. He was freed of the steel links on his wrists and pushed inside; he heard the door shut behind him.

'Sit down, Bigger. Say, how do you feel?'

Bigger sat down on the edge of the chair and did not answer. The room was small. A single yellow electric globe dropped from the ceiling. There was one barred window. All about them was profound silence. Max sat opposite Bigger, and Bigger's eyes met his and fell. Bigger felt that he was sitting and holding his life helplessly in his hands, waiting for Max to tell him what to do with it; and it made him hate himself. An organic wish to cease to be, to stop living, seized him. Either he was too weak, or the world was too strong; he did not know which. Over and over he had tried to create a world to live in, and over and over he had failed. Now, once again, he was waiting for someone to tell him something; once more he was poised on the verge of action and commitment. Was he letting himself in for more hate and fear? What could Max do for him now? Even if Max tried hard and honestly, were there not thousands of white hands to stop Max? Why not tell him to go home? His lips trembled to speak, to tell Max to leave; but no words came. He felt that even in speaking in that way he would be indicating how hopeless he felt, thereby disrobing his soul to more shame.

'I bought some clothes for you,' Max said. 'When they give 'em to you in the morning, put 'em on. You want to look your best when you come up for arraignment.'

Bigger was silent; he glanced at Max again, and then away.

'What's on your mind, Bigger?'

'Nothing,' he mumbled.

'Now, listen, Bigger. I want you to tell me all about yourself . . .'

'Mr Max, it ain't no use in you doing nothing!' Bigger blurted.

Max eyed him sharply.

'Do you really feel that way, Bigger?'

'There ain't no way else to feel.'

'I want to talk to you honestly, Bigger. I see no way out of this but a plea of guilty. We can ask for mercy, for life in prison . . .'

'I'd rather die!'

'Nonsense. You want to live.'

'For what?'

'Don't you want to fight this thing?'

'What can I do? They got me.'

'You don't want to die that way, Bigger.'

'It don't matter which way I die,' he said; but his voice choked.

'Listen, Bigger, you're facing a sea of hate now that's no different from what you've faced all your life. And because it's that way, you've *got* to fight. If they can wipe you out, then they can wipe others out, too.'

'Yeah,' Bigger mumbled, resting his hands upon his knees and staring at the black floor. 'But I can't win.'

'First of all, Bigger. Do you trust me?'

Bigger grew angry.

'You can't help me, Mr Max,' he said, looking straight into Max's eyes.

'But do you trust me, Bigger?' Max asked again.

Bigger looked away. He felt that Max was making it very difficult for him to tell him to leave.

'I don't know, Mr Max.'

'Bigger, I know my face is white,' Max said. 'And I know that almost every white face you've met in your life had it in for you, even when that white face didn't know it. Every white man considers it his duty to make a black man keep his distance. He doesn't know why most of the time, but he acts that way. It's the way things are, Bigger. But I want you to know that you can trust me.'

'It ain't no use, Mr Max.'

'You want me to handle your case?'

'You can't help me none. They got me.'

Bigger knew that Max was trying to make him feel that he accepted the way he looked at things and it made him as self-conscious as when Jan had taken his hand and shaken it that night in the car. It made him live again in that hard and sharp consciousness of his color and feel that shame and fear that went with it, and at the same time it made him hate himself for feeling it. He trusted Max. Was Max not taking upon himself a thing that would make other whites hate him? But he doubted if Max could make him see things in a way that would enable him to go to his death. He doubted that God Himself could give him a picture for that now. As he felt at present, they would have to drag him to the chair, as they had dragged him down the steps the night they captured him. He did not want his feelings tampered with; he feared that he might walk into another trap. If he expressed belief in Max, if he acted on that belief, would it not end just as all other commitments of faith had ended? He wanted to believe; but was afraid. He felt that he should have been able to meet Max halfway; but, as always, when a white man talked to him, he was caught out in No Man's Land. He sat slumped in his chair with his head down and he looked at Max only when Max's eyes were not watching him.

'Here; take a cigarette, Bigger.' Max lit Bigger's and then lit his own; they smoked awhile. 'Bigger, I'm your lawyer. I want to talk to you honestly. What you say is in strictest confidence . . .'

Bigger stared at Max. He felt sorry for the white man. He saw that Max was afraid that he would not talk at all. And he had no desire to hurt Max. Max leaned forward determinedly. Well, tell him. Talk. Get it over with and let Max go.

'Aw, I don't care what I say or do now . . .'

'Oh, yes, you *do*!' Max said quickly.

In a fleeting second an impulse to laugh rose up in Bigger, and left. Max was anxious to help him and he had to die.

'Maybe I do care,' Bigger drawled.

'If you don't care about what you say or do, then why didn't you re-enact that crime out at the Dalton home today?'

'I wouldn't do nothing for *them*.'

'Why?'

'They hate black folks,' he said.

'*Why*, Bigger?'

'I don't know, Mr Max.'

'Bigger, don't you know they hate others, too?'

'Who they hate?'

'They hate trade unions. They hate folks who try to organize. They hate Jan.'

'But they hate black folks more than they hate unions,' Bigger said. 'They don't treat union folks like they do me.'

'Oh, yes, they do. You think that because your color makes it easy for them to point you out, segregate you, exploit you. But they do that to others, too. They hate me because I'm trying to help you. They're writing me letters, calling me a "dirty Jew".'

'All I know is that they hate me,' Bigger said grimly.

'Bigger, the State's Attorney gave me a copy of your confession. Now, tell me, did you tell him the truth?'

'Yeah. There wasn't nothing else to do.'

'Now, tell me this, Bigger. Why did you do it?' Bigger sighed, shrugged his shoulders and sucked his lungs full of smoke.

'I don't know,' he said; smoke eddied slowly from his nostrils.

'Did you plan it?'

'Naw.'

'Did anybody help you?'

'Naw.'

'Had you been thinking about doing something like that for a long time?'

'Naw.'

'How did it happen?'

'It just happened, Mr Max.'

'Are you sorry?'

'What's the use of being sorry? That won't help me none.'

'You can't think of any reason why you did it?'

Bigger was staring straight before him, his eyes wide and shining. His talking to Max had evoked again in him that urge to talk, to tell, to try to make his feelings known. A wave of excitement flooded him. He felt that he ought to be able to reach out with his bare hands and carve from

naked space the concrete, solid reasons why he had murdered. He felt them that strongly. If he could do that, he
would relax; he would sit and wait until they told him to
walk to the chair; and he would walk.

'Mr Max, I don't know. I was all mixed up. I was feeling
so many things at once.'

'Did you rape her, Bigger?'

'Naw, Mr Max. I didn't. But nobody'll believe me.'

'Had you planned to before Mrs Dalton came into the
room?'

Bigger shook his head and rubbed his hands nervously
across his eyes. In a sense he had forgotten Max was in the
room. He was trying to feel the texture of his own feelings, trying to tell what they meant.

'Oh, I don't know. I was feeling a little that way. Yeah,
I reckon I was. I was drunk and she was drunk and I was
feeling that way.'

'But, did you rape her?'

'Naw. But everybody'll say I did. What's the use? I'm
black. They say black men do that. So it don't matter if I
did or if I didn't.'

'How long had you known her?'

'A few hours.'

'Did you like her?'

'*Like* her?'

Bigger's voice boomed so suddenly from his throat that
Max started. Bigger leaped to his feet; his eyes widened
and his hands lifted midway to his face, trembling.

'No! No! Bigger . . .' Max said.

'*Like* her? I *hated* her! So help me God, I hated her!' he shouted.

'Sit down, Bigger!'

'I hate her now, even though she's dead! God knows, I hate her right now . . .'

Max grabbed him and pushed him back into the chair.

'Don't get excited, Bigger. Here; take it easy!'

Bigger quieted, but his eyes roved the room. Finally, he lowered his head and knotted his fingers. His lips were slightly parted.

'You say you hated her?'

'Yeah; and I ain't sorry she's dead.'

'But what had she done to you? You say you had just met her.'

'I don't know. She didn't do nothing to me.' He paused and ran his hand nervously across his forehead. 'She . . . It was . . . Hell, I don't know. She asked me a lot of questions. She acted and talked in a way that made me hate her. She made me feel like a dog. I was so mad I wanted to cry . . .' His voice trailed off in a plaintive whimper. He licked his lips. He was caught in a net of vague, associative memory: he saw an image of his little sister, Vera, sitting on the edge of a chair crying because he had shamed her by 'looking' at her; he saw her rise and fling her shoe at him. He shook his head, confused. 'Aw, Mr Max, she wanted me to tell her how Negroes live. She got into the front seat of the car where I was . . .'

'But, Bigger, you don't hate people for that. She was being kind to you . . .'

'Kind, hell! She wasn't kind to me!'

'What do you mean? She accepted you as another human being.'

'Mr Max, we're all split up. What you say is kind ain't kind at all. I didn't know nothing about that woman. All I knew was that they kill us for women like her. We live apart. And then she comes and acts like that to me.'

'Bigger, you should have tried to understand. She was acting toward you only as she knew how.'

Bigger glared about the small room, searching for an answer. He knew that his actions did not seem logical and he gave up trying to explain them logically. He reverted to his feelings as a guide in answering Max.

'Well, I acted toward her only as I know how. She was rich. She and her kind own the earth. She and her kind say black folks are dogs. They don't let you do nothing but what they want . . .'

'But, Bigger, *this* woman was trying to help you!'

'She didn't act like it.'

'How *should* she have acted?'

'Aw, I don't know, Mr Max. White folks and black folks is strangers. We don't know what each other is thinking. Maybe she was trying to be kind; but she didn't act like it. To me she looked and acted like all other white folks . . .'

'But she's not to be blamed for that, Bigger.'

'She's the same color as the rest of 'em,' he said defensively.

'I don't understand, Bigger. You say you hated her and yet you say you felt like having her when you were in the room and she was drunk and you were drunk . . .'

'Yeah,' Bigger said, wagging his head and wiping his mouth with the back of his hand. 'Yeah; that's funny, ain't it?' He sucked at his cigarette. 'Yeah; I reckon it was because I knew I oughtn't've wanted to. I reckon it was because they say we black men do that anyhow. Mr Max, you know what some white men say we black men do? They say we rape white women when we got the clap and they say we do that because we believe that if we rape white women then we'll get rid of the clap. That's what some white men *say*. They *believe* that. Jesus, Mr Max, when folks says things like that about you, you whipped before you born. What's the use? Yeah; I reckon I was feeling that way when I was in the room with her. They say we do things like that and they say it to kill us. They draw a line and say for you to stay on your side of the line. They don't care if there's no bread over on your side. They don't care if you die. And then they say things like that about you and when you try to come from behind your line they kill you. They feel they ought to kill you then. Everybody wants to kill you then. Yeah; I reckon I was feeling that way and maybe the reason was because they say it. Maybe that was the reason.'

'You mean you wanted to defy them? You wanted to show them that you dared, that you didn't care?'

'I don't know, Mr Max. But what I got to care about? I knew that some time or other they was going to get me for something. I'm black. I don't have to do nothing for 'em to get me. The first white finger they point at me, I'm a goner, see?'

'But, Bigger, when Mrs Dalton came into that room, why didn't you stop right there and tell her what was wrong? You wouldn't've been in all this trouble then . . .'

'Mr Max, so help me God, I couldn't do nothing when I turned around and saw that woman coming to that bed. Honest to God, I didn't know what I was doing . . .'

'You mean you went blank?'

'Naw; naw . . . I knew what I was doing, all right. But I couldn't help it. That's what I mean. It was like another man stepped inside of my skin and started acting for me . . .'

'Bigger, tell me, did you feel more attraction for Mary than for the women of your own race?'

'Naw. But they say that. It ain't true. I hated her then and I hate her now.'

'But why did you kill Bessie?'

'To keep her from talking. Mr Max, after killing that white woman, it wasn't hard to kill somebody else. I didn't have to think much about killing Bessie. I knew I had to kill her and I did. I had to get away . . .'

'Did you hate Bessie?'

'Naw.'

'Did you love her?'

'Naw. I was just scared. I wasn't in love with Bessie. She

was just my girl. I don't reckon I was ever in love with nobody. I killed Bessie to save myself. You have to have a girl, so I had Bessie. And I killed her.'

'Bigger, tell me, when did you start hating Mary?'

'I hated her as soon as she spoke to me, as soon as I saw her. I reckon I hated her before I saw her . . .'

'But, *why*?'

'I told you. What her kind ever let us do?'

'What, exactly, Bigger, did you want to do?'

Bigger sighed and sucked at his cigarette.

'Nothing, I reckon. Nothing. But I reckon I wanted to do what other people do.'

'And because you couldn't, you hated her?'

Again Bigger felt that his actions were not logical, and again he fell back upon his feelings for a guide in answering Max's questions.

'Mr Max, a guy gets tired of being told what he can do and can't do. You get a little job here and a little job there. You shine shoes, sweep streets; anything . . . You don't make enough to live on. You don't know when you going to get fired. Pretty soon you get so you can't hope for nothing. You just keep moving all the time, doing what other folks say. You ain't a man no more. You just work day in and day out so the world can roll on and other people can live. You know, Mr Max, I always think of white folks . . .'

He paused. Max leaned forward and touched him.

'Go on, Bigger.'

'Well, they own everything. They choke you off the

face of the earth. They like God . . .' He swallowed, closed his eyes and sighed. 'They don't even let you feel what you want to feel. They after you so hot and hard you can only feel what they doing to you. They kill you before you die.'

'But, Bigger, I asked you what it was that you wanted to do so badly that you had to hate them?'

'Nothing. I reckon I didn't want to do nothing.'

'But you said that people like Mary and her kind never let you do anything.'

'Why should I want to do anything? I ain't got a chance. I don't know nothing. I'm just black and they make the laws.'

'What would you like to have been?'

Bigger was silent for a long time. Then he laughed without sound, without moving his lips; it was three short expulsions of breath forced upward through his nostrils by the heaving of his chest.

'I wanted to be an aviator once. But they wouldn't let me go to the school where I was suppose' to learn it. They built a big school and then drew a line around it and said that nobody could go to it but those who lived within the line. That kept all the colored boys out.'

'And what else?'

'Well, I wanted to be in the army once.'

'Why didn't you join?'

'Hell, it's a Jim Crow army. All they want a black man for is to dig ditches. And in the navy, all I can do is wash dishes and scrub floors.'

'And was there anything else you wanted to do?'

'Oh, I don't know. What's the use now? I'm through, washed up. They got me. I'll die.'

'Tell me the things you *thought* you'd have liked to do?'

'I'd like to be in business. But what chance has a black guy got in business? We ain't got no money. We don't own no mines, no railroads, no nothing. They don't want us to. They made us stay in one little spot . . .'

'And you didn't want to stay there?'

Bigger glanced up; his lips tightened. There was a feverish pride in his bloodshot eyes.

'I *didn't*,' he said.

\*

WHEN MAX CAME Bigger saw that his face was pale and drawn. There were dark rings beneath the eyes. Max laid a hand on Bigger's knee and whispered,

'I'm going to do all I can, son.'

Court opened and the judge said,

'Are you ready to proceed, Mr Max?'

'Yes, Your Honor.'

Max rose, ran his hand through his white hair and went to the front of the room. He turned and half-faced the judge and Buckley, looking out over Bigger's head to the crowd. He cleared his throat.

'Your Honor, never in my life have I risen in court to make a plea with a firmer conviction in my heart. I know that what I have to say here today touches the destiny of an entire nation. My plea is for more than one man and one people. Perhaps it is in a manner fortunate that the defendant has committed one of the darkest crimes in our memory; for if we can encompass the life of this man and find out what has happened to him, if we can understand how subtly and yet strongly his life and fate are linked to ours – if we can do this, perhaps we shall find the key to our future, that rare vantage point upon which every man and woman in this nation can stand and view how inextricably our hopes and fears of today create the exultation and doom of tomorrow.

'Your Honor, I have no desire to be disrespectful to this Court, but I must be honest. A man's life is at stake. And not only is this man a criminal, but he is a black criminal. And as such, he comes into this court under a handicap, notwithstanding our pretensions that all are equal before the law.

'This man is *different*, even though his crime differs from similar crimes only in degree. The complex forces of society have isolated here for us a symbol, a test symbol. The prejudices of men have stained this symbol, like a germ stained for examination under the microscope. The unremitting hate of men has given us a psychological distance that will enable us to see this tiny social symbol in relation to our whole sick social organism.

'I say, Your Honor, that the mere act of understanding Bigger Thomas will be a thawing out of icebound impulses, a dragging of the sprawling forms of dread out of the night of fear into the light of reason, an unveiling of the unconscious ritual of death in which we, like sleep-walkers, have participated so dreamlike and thoughtlessly.

'But I make no excessive claims, Your Honor. I do not deal in magic. I do not say that if we understand this man's life we shall solve all our problems, or that when we have all the facts at our disposal we shall automatically know how to act. Life is not that simple. But I do say that, if, after I have finished, you feel that death is necessary, then you are making an open choice. What I want to do is inject the consciousness of this Court, through the discussion of evidence, the two possible courses of action open to us and the inevitable consequences flowing from each. And then, if we say death, let us mean it; and if we say life, let us mean that too; but whatever we say, let us know upon what ground we are putting our feet, what the consequences are for us and those whom we judge.

'Your Honor, I would have you believe that I am not insensible to the deep burden of responsibility I am throwing upon your shoulders by the manner in which I have insisted upon conducting the defense of this boy's life, and in my resolve to place before you the entire degree of his guilt for judgment. But, under the circumstances, what else could I have done? Night after night, I have lain without sleep, trying to think of a way to picture to you and to the world the causes and reasons why this Negro boy sits here a self-confessed murderer. How can I,

I asked myself, make the picture of what has happened to this boy show plain and powerful upon a screen of sober reason, when a thousand newspaper and magazine artists have already drawn it in lurid ink upon a million sheets of public print? Dare I, deeply mindful of this boy's background and race, put his fate in the hands of a jury (not of his peers, but of an alien and hostile race!) whose minds are already conditioned by the press of the nation; a press which has already reached a decision as to his guilt, and in countless editorials suggested the measure of his punishment?

'No! I could not! So today I come to face this Court, rejecting a trial by jury, willingly entering a plea of guilty, asking in the light of the laws of this state that this boy's life be spared for reasons which I believe affect the foundations of our civilization.

'The most habitual thing for this Court to do is to take the line of least resistance and follow the suggestion of the State's Attorney and say, "Death!" And that would be the end of this case. But that would not be the end of this crime! That is why this Court must do otherwise.

'There are times, Your Honor, when reality bears features of such an impellingly moral complexion that it is impossible to follow the hewn path of expediency. There are times when life's ends are so raveled that reason and sense cry out that we stop and gather them together again before we can proceed.

'What atmosphere surrounds this trial? Are the

citizens soberly intent upon seeing that the law is executed? That retribution is dealt out in measure with the offense? That the guilty and only the guilty is caught and punished?

'No! Every conceivable prejudice has been dragged into this case. The authorities of the city and state deliberately inflamed the public mind to the point where they could not keep the peace without martial law. Responsible to nothing but their own corrupt conscience, the newspapers and the prosecution launched the ridiculous claim that the Communist Party was in some way linked to these two murders. Only here in court yesterday morning did the State's Attorney cease implying that Bigger Thomas was guilty of other crimes, crimes which he could not prove.

'The hunt for Bigger Thomas served as an excuse to terrorize the entire Negro population, to arrest hundreds of Communists, to raid labor union headquarters and workers' organizations. Indeed, the tone of the press, the silence of the church, the attitude of the prosecution, and the stimulated temper of the people are of such a nature as to indicate that *more* than revenge is being sought upon a man who has committed a crime.

'What is the cause of all this high feeling and excitement? Is it the crime of Bigger Thomas? Were Negroes liked yesterday and hated today because of what he has done? Were labor unions and workers' halls raided solely because a Negro committed a crime? Did those white bones lying on that table evoke the gasp of horror that went up from the nation?

'Your Honor, you know that that is *not* the case! All of the factors in the present hysteria existed before Bigger Thomas was ever heard of. Negroes, workers, and labor unions were hated as much yesterday as they are today.

'Crimes of even greater brutality and horror have been committed in this city. Gangsters have killed and have gone free to kill again. But none of that brought forth an indignation to equal this.

'Your Honor, that mob did not come here of its own accord! It was *incited*! Until a week ago those people lived their lives as quietly as always.

'Who, then, fanned this latent hate into fury? Whose interest is that thoughtless and misguided mob serving?

'The State's Attorney knows, for he promised the Loop bankers that if he were re-elected demonstrations for relief would be stopped! The Governor of the State knows, for he has pledged the Manufacturers' Association that he would use troops against workers who went out on strike! The Mayor knows, for he told the merchants of the city that the budget would be cut down, that no new taxes would be imposed to satisfy the clamor of the masses of the needy!

'There is guilt in the rage that demands that this man's life be snuffed out quickly! There is fear in the hate and impatience which impels the action of the mob congregated upon the streets beyond that window! All of them – the mob and the mob-masters; the wire-pullers and the frightened; the leaders and their pet vassals – know and feel that their lives are built upon a historical deed of wrong against many people, people from whose lives they have bled their leisure and their luxury! Their feeling of guilt is as deep as that of the boy who sits here on trial today. Fear and hate and guilt are the keynotes of this drama!

'Your Honor, for the sake of this boy and myself, I wish I could bring to this Court evidence of a morally worthier nature, I wish I could say that love, ambition, jealousy, the quest for adventure, or any of the more romantic feelings were back of these two murders. If I could honestly invest the hapless actor in this fateful drama with feelings of a loftier cast, my task would be easier and I would feel confident of the outcome. The odds would be with me, for I would be appealing to men bound by common ideals to judge with pity and understanding one of their brothers who erred and fell in struggle. But I have no choice in this matter. Life has cut this cloth; not I.

'We must deal here with the raw stuff of life, emotions and impulses and attitudes as yet unconditioned by the strivings of science and civilization. We must deal here with a first wrong which, when committed by us, was understandable and inevitable; and then we must deal with the long trailing black sense of guilt stemming from that wrong, a sense of guilt which self-interest and fear would not let us atone. And we must deal here with the hot blasts of hate engendered in others by that first wrong, and then the monstrous and horrible crimes flowing from that hate, a hate which has seeped down into the hearts and molded the deepest and most delicate sensibilities of multitudes.

'We must deal here with a dislocation of life involving millions of people, a dislocation so vast as to stagger the imagination; so fraught with tragic consequences as to make us rather not want to look at it or think of it; so old that we would rather try to view it as an order of nature and strive with uneasy conscience and false moral fervor to keep it so.

'We must deal here, on both sides of the fence, among whites as well as blacks, among workers as well as employers, with men and women in whose minds there loom good and bad of such height and weight that they assume proportions of abnormal aspect and construction. When situations like this arise, instead of men feeling that they are facing other men, they feel that they are facing mountains, floods, seas: forces of nature whose size and strength focus the minds and emotions to a degree of tension unusual in the quiet routine of urban life. Yet this tension exists within the limits of urban life, undermining it and supporting it in the same gesture of being.

'Allow me, Your Honor, before I proceed to cast blame and ask for mercy, to state emphatically that I do *not* claim that this boy is a victim of injustice, nor do I ask that this Court be sympathetic with him. That is not my object in embracing his character and his cause. It is not to tell you only of suffering that I stand here today, even though there are frequent lynchings and floggings of Negroes throughout the country. If you react only to that part of what I say, then you, too, are caught as much as he in the mire of blind emotion, and this vicious game will roll on, like a bloody river to a bloodier sea. Let us banish from our minds the thought that this is an unfortunate victim of injustice. The very concept of injustice rests upon a premise of equal claims, and this boy here today makes no claim upon you. If you think or feel that he does, then you, too, are blinded by a feeling as terrible as that which you condemn in him, and without as much justification. The feeling of guilt which has caused all of the mob-fear and mob-hysteria is the counterpart of his own hate.

'Rather, I plead with you to see a mode of *life* in our midst, a mode of life stunted and distorted, but possessing its own laws and claims, an existence of men growing out of the soil prepared by the collective but blind will of a hundred million people. I beg you to recognize human life draped in a form and guise alien to ours, but springing from a soil plowed and sown by all our hands. I ask you to recognize the laws and processes flowing from such a condition, understand them, seek to change them. If we do none of these, then we should not pretend horror or surprise when thwarted life expresses itself in fear and hate and crime.

'This is life, new and strange; strange, because we fear

**Injustice rests upon a premise of equal claims, and this boy here today makes no claims upon you**

it; new, because we have kept our eyes turned from it. This is life lived in cramped limits and expressing itself not in terms of our good and bad, but in terms of its own fulfillment. Men are men and life is life, and we must deal with them as they are: and if we want to change them, we must deal with them in the form in which they exist and have their being.

'Your Honor, I must still speak in general terms, for the background of this boy must be shown, a background which has acted powerfully and importantly upon his conduct. Our forefathers came to these shores and faced a harsh and wild country. They came here with a stifled dream in their hearts, from lands where their personalities had been denied, as even we have denied the personality of this boy. They came from cities of the old world where the means to sustain life were hard to get or own. They were colonists and they were faced with a difficult choice: they had either to subdue this wild land or be subdued by it. We need but turn our eyes upon the imposing sweep of streets and factories and buildings to see how completely they have conquered. But in conquering they *used* others, used their lives. Like a miner using a pick or a carpenter using a saw, they bent the will of others to their own. Lives to them were tools and weapons to be wielded against a hostile land and climate.

'I do not say this in terms of moral condemnation. I do not say it to rouse pity in you for the black men who were slaves for two and one-half centuries. It would be foolish now to look back upon that in the light of injustice. Let us not be naïve: men do what they must, even when they feel that they are being driven by God, even when they feel they are fulfilling the will of God. Those men were engaged in a struggle for life and their choice in the matter was small indeed. It was the imperial dream of a feudal age that made men enslave others. Exalted by the will to rule, they could not have built nations on so vast a scale had they not shut their eyes to the humanity of other men, men whose lives were necessary for their building. But the invention and widespread use of machines made the further direct enslavement of men economically impossible, and so slavery ended.

'Let me, Your Honor, dwell a moment longer upon the danger of looking upon this boy in the light of injustice. If I should say that he is a victim of injustice, then I would be asking by implication for sympathy; and if one insists upon looking at this boy in the light of sympathy, he will be swamped by a feeling of guilt so strong as to be indistinguishable from hate.

'Of all things, men do not like to feel that they are guilty of wrong, and if you make them feel guilt, they will try desperately to justify it on any grounds; but, failing that, and seeing no immediate solution that will set things right without too much cost to their lives and property, they will kill that which evoked in them the condemning sense of guilt. And this is true of all men, whether they be white or black; it is a peculiar and powerful, but common, need.

'This guilt-fear is the basic tone of the prosecution and of the people in this case. In their hearts they feel that a wrong has been done and when a Negro commits a crime against them, they fancy they see the ghastly evidence of that wrong. So the men of wealth and property, the victims of attack who are eager to protect their profits, say to their guilty hirelings, "Stamp out this ghost!" Or, like Mr Dalton, they say, "Let's do something for this man so he won't feel that way." But then it is too late.

'If only ten or twenty Negroes had been put into slavery, we could call it injustice, but there were hundreds of thousands of them throughout the country. If this state of affairs had lasted for two or three years, we could say that it was unjust; but it lasted for more than two hundred years. Injustice which lasts for three long centuries and which exists among millions of people over thousands of square miles of territory, is injustice no longer; it is an accomplished fact of life. Men adjust themselves to their land; they create their own laws of being; their notions of right and wrong. A common way of earning a living gives them a common attitude toward life. Even their speech is colored and shaped by what they must undergo. Your Honor, injustice blots out one form of life, but another grows up in its place with its own rights, needs, and aspirations. What is happening here today is not injustice, but *oppression*, an attempt to throttle or stamp out a new form of life. And it is this new form of life that has grown up here in our midst that puzzles us, that expresses itself, like a weed growing from under a stone, in terms we call crime. Unless we grasp this problem in the light of this new reality, we cannot do more than salve our feelings of guilt and rage with more murder when a man, living under such conditions, commits an act which we call a crime.

'This boy represents but a tiny aspect of a problem whose reality sprawls over a third of this nation. Kill him! Burn the life out of him! And still when the delicate and unconscious machinery of race relations slips, there will be murder again. How can law contradict the lives of millions of people and hope to be administered successfully? Do we believe in magic? Do you believe that by burning a cross you can frighten a multitude, paralyze their will and impulses? Do you think that the white daughters in the homes of America will be any safer if you kill this boy? No! I tell you in all solemnity that they won't! The surest way to make certain that there will be more such murders is to kill this boy. In your rage and guilt, make thousands of other black men and women feel that the barriers are tighter and higher! Kill him and swell the tide of pent-up lava that will some day break loose, not in a single, blundering, accidental, individual crime, but in a wild cataract of emotion that will brook no control. The all-important thing for this Court to remember in deciding this boy's fate is that, though his crime was accidental, the emotions that broke loose were *already* there; the thing to remember is that this boy's way of life was a way of guilt; that his crime existed long before the murder of Mary Dalton; that the accidental nature of his crime took the guise of a sudden and violent rent in the veil behind which he lived, a rent which allowed his feelings of resentment and estrangement to leap forth and find objective and concrete form.

'Obsessed with guilt, we have sought to thrust a corpse from before our eyes. We have marked off a little plot of ground and buried it. We tell our souls in the deep of the black night that it is dead and that we have no reason for fear or uneasiness.

'But the corpse returns and raids our homes! We find our daughters murdered and burnt! And we say, "Kill! Kill!"

'But, Your Honor, I say: "Stop! Let us look at what we are doing!" For the corpse is not dead! It still lives! It has made itself a home in the wild forest of our great cities, amid the rank and choking vegetation of slums! It has forgotten our language! In order to live it has sharpened its claws! It has grown hard and calloused! It has developed a capacity for hate and fury which we cannot understand! Its movements are unpredictable! By night it creeps from its lair and steals toward the settlements of civilization! And at the sight of a kind face it does not lie down upon its back and kick up its heels playfully to be tickled and stroked. No; it leaps to kill!

'Yes, Mary Dalton, a well-intentioned white girl with a smile upon her face, came to Bigger Thomas to help him. Mr Dalton, feeling vaguely that a social wrong existed, wanted to give him a job so that his family could eat and his sister and brother could go to school. Mrs Dalton, trying to grope her way toward a sense of decency, wanted him to go to school and learn a trade. But when they stretched forth their helping hands, death struck! Today they mourn and wait for revenge. The wheel of blood continues to turn!

*

SLOWLY, BIGGER TURNED and came back to the cot. He stood before Max again, about to speak, his right hand raised. Then he sat down and bowed his head.

'What is it, Bigger? Is there anything you want me to do on the outside? Any message you want to send?'

'Naw,' he breathed.

'What's on your mind?'

'I don't know.'

He could not talk. Max reached over and placed a hand on his shoulder, and Bigger could tell by its touch that Max did not know, had no suspicion of what he wanted, of what he was trying to say. Max was upon another planet, far off in space. Was there any way to break down this wall of isolation? Distractedly, he gazed about the cell, trying to remember where he had heard words that would help him. He could recall none. He had lived outside of the lives of men. Their modes of communication, their symbols and images, had been denied him. Yet Max had given him the faith that at bottom all men lived as he lived and felt as he felt. And of all the men he had met, surely Max knew what he was trying to say. Had Max left him? Had Max, knowing that he was to die, thrust him from his thoughts and feelings, assigned him to the grave? Was he already numbered among the dead? His lips quivered and his eyes grew misty. Yes; Max had left him. Max was not a friend. Anger welled in him. But he knew that anger was useless.

Max rose and went to a small window; a pale bar of sunshine fell across his white head. And Bigger, looking at him, saw that sunshine for the first time in many days; and as he saw it, the entire cell, with its four close walls, became crushingly real. He glanced down at himself; the shaft of yellow sun cut across his chest with as much weight as a beam forged of lead. With a convulsive gasp, he bent forward and shut his eyes. It was not a white mountain looming over him now; Gus was not whistling 'The Merry-Go-Round Broke Down' as he came into Doc's poolroom to make him go and rob Blum's; he was not standing over Mary's bed with the white blur hovering near; – this new adversary did not make him taut; it sapped strength and left him weak. He summoned his energies and lifted his head and struck out desperately, determined to rise from the grave, resolved to force upon Max the reality of his living.

'I'm glad I got to know you before I go!' he said with almost a shout; then was silent, for that was not what he had wanted to say.

Max turned and looked at him; it was a casual look, devoid of the deeper awareness that Bigger sought so hungrily.

'I'm glad I got to know you, too, Bigger. I'm sorry we have to part this way. But I'm old, son. I'll be going soon myself . . .'

'I remembered all them questions you asked me . . .'

'What questions?' Max asked, coming and sitting again on the cot.

'That night . . .'

'What night, son?'

Max did not even *know*! Bigger felt that he had been slapped. Oh, what a fool he had been to build hope upon such shifting sand! But he had to *make* him know!

'That night you asked me to tell all about myself,' he whimpered despairingly.

'Oh.'

He saw Max look at the floor and frown. He knew that Max was puzzled.

'You asked me questions nobody ever asked me before. You knew that I was a murderer two times over, but you treated me like a man . . .'

Max looked at him sharply and rose from his cot. He stood in front of Bigger for a moment and Bigger was on the verge of believing that Max knew, understood; but Max's next words showed him that the white man was still trying to comfort him in the face of death.

'You're human, Bigger,' Max said wearily. 'It's hell to

talk about things like this to one about to die . . .' Max paused; Bigger knew that he was searching for words that would soothe him, and he did not want them. 'Bigger,' Max said, 'in the work I'm doing, I look at the world in a way that shows no whites and no blacks, no civilized and no savages . . . When men are trying to change human life on earth, those little things don't matter. You don't notice 'em. They're just not there. You forget them. The reason I spoke to you as I did, Bigger, is because you made me feel how badly men want to live . . .'

'But sometimes I wish you hadn't asked me them questions,' Bigger said in a voice that had as much reproach in it for Max as it had for himself.

'What do you mean, Bigger?'

'They made me think and thinking's made me scared a little . . .'

Max caught Bigger's shoulders in a tight grip; then his fingers loosened and Bigger sank back to the cot; but his eyes were still fastened upon Bigger's face. Yes; Max knew now. Under the shadow of death, he wanted Max to tell him about life.

'Mr Max, how can I die!' Bigger asked; knowing as the words boomed from his lips that a knowledge of how to live was a knowledge of how to die.

Max turned his face from him, and mumbled,

'Men die alone, Bigger.'

But Bigger had not heard him. In him again, imperiously, was the desire to talk, to tell; his hands were lifted in mid-air and when he spoke he tried to charge into the tone of his words what he *himself* wanted to hear, what *he* needed.

'Mr Max, I sort of saw myself after that night. And I sort of saw other people, too.' Bigger's voice died; he was listening to the echoes of his words in his own mind. He saw amazement and horror on Max's face. Bigger knew that Max would rather not have him talk like this; but he could not help it. He had to die and he had to talk. 'Well, it's sort of funny, Mr Max. I ain't trying to dodge what's coming to me.' Bigger was growing hysterical. 'I know I'm going to get it. I'm going to die. Well, that's all right now. But really I never wanted to hurt nobody. That's the truth, Mr Max. I hurt folk 'cause I felt I had to; that's all. They was crowding me too close; they wouldn't give me no room. Lots of times I tried to forget 'em, but I couldn't. They wouldn't let me . . .' Bigger's eyes were wide and unseeing; his voice rushed on; 'Mr Max, I didn't mean to do what I did. I was trying to do something else. But it seems like I never could. I was always wanting something and I was feeling that nobody would let me have it. So I fought 'em. I thought they was hard and I acted hard.' He paused, then whimpered in confession, 'But I ain't hard, Mr Max. I ain't hard even a little bit . . .' He rose to his feet. 'But . . . I – I won't be crying none when they take me to that chair. But I'll b-b-be feeling inside of me like I was crying . . . I'll be feeling and thinking that they didn't see me and I didn't see them . . .' He ran to the steel door and caught the bars in his hands and shook them, as though trying to tear the steel from its concrete moorings. Max went to him and grabbed his shoulders.

'Bigger,' Max said helplessly.

Bigger grew still and leaned weakly against the door.

'Mr Max, I know the folks who sent me here to die hated me; I know that. B-b-but you reckon th-they was like m-me, trying to g-get something like I was, and when I'm dead and gone they'll be saying like I'm saying now that they didn't mean to hurt nobody . . . th-that they were t-trying to get something, too . . . ?'

Max did not answer. Bigger saw a look of indecision and wonder come into the old man's eyes.

'Tell me, Mr Max. You think they was?'

'Bigger,' Max pleaded.

'*Tell* me, Mr Max!'

Max shook his head and mumbled,

'You're asking me to say things I don't want to say . . .'

'But I want to *know*!'

'You're going to die, Bigger . . .'

Max's voice faded. Bigger knew that the old man had not wanted to say that; he had said it because he had pushed him, had made him say it. They were silent for a moment longer, then Bigger whispered,

'That's why I want to know . . . I reckon it's 'cause I know I'm going to die that makes me want to know . . .'

Max's face was ashy. Bigger feared that he was going to leave. Across a gulf of silence, they looked at each other. Max sighed.

'Come here, Bigger,' he said.

He followed Max to the window and saw in the distance the tips of sun-drenched buildings in the Loop.

'See all those buildings, Bigger?' Max asked, placing an arm about Bigger's shoulders. He spoke hurriedly, as though trying to mold a substance which was warm and pliable, but which might soon cool.

'Yeah. I see 'em . . .'

'You lived in one of them once, Bigger. They're made out of steel and stone. But the steel and stone don't hold 'em together. You know what holds those buildings up, Bigger? You know what keeps them in their place, keeps them from tumbling down?'

Bigger looked at him, bewildered.

'It's the belief of men. If men stopped believing, stopped having faith, they'd come tumbling down. Those buildings sprang up out of the hearts of men, Bigger. Men like you. Men kept hungry, kept needing, and those buildings kept growing and unfolding. You once told me you wanted to do a lot of things. Well, that's the feeling that keeps those buildings in their places . . .'

'You mean . . . You talking about what I said that night, when I said I wanted to do a lot of things?' Bigger's voice came quiet, childlike in its tone of hungry wonder.

'Yes. What you felt, what you wanted, is what keeps those buildings standing there. When millions of men are desiring and longing, those buildings grow and unfold. But, Bigger, those buildings aren't growing any more. A few men are squeezing those buildings tightly in their hands. The buildings can't unfold, can't feed the dreams men have, men like you . . . The men on the inside of those buildings have begun to doubt, just as you did. They don't believe any more. They don't feel it's their world. They're restless, like you, Bigger. They have nothing. There's nothing through which they can grow and unfold. They go in the streets and they stand outside of those buildings and look and wonder . . .'

'B-b-but what they hate me for?' Bigger asked.

'The men who own those buildings are afraid. They want to keep what they own, even if it makes others suffer. In order to keep it, they push men down in the mud and tell them that they are beasts. But men, men like you, get angry and fight to re-enter those buildings, to live again. Bigger, you killed. That was wrong. That was not the way to do it. It's too late now for you to . . . work with . . . others who are t-trying to . . . believe and make the world live again . . . But it's not too late to believe what you felt, to understand what you felt . . .'

Bigger was gazing in the direction of the buildings; but he did not see them. He was trying to react to the picture Max was drawing, trying to compare that picture with what he had felt all his life.

'I always wanted to do something,' he mumbled.

They were silent and Max did not speak again until Bigger looked at him. Max closed his eyes.

'Bigger, you're going to die. And if you die, die free.

You're trying to believe in yourself. And every time you try to find a way to live, your own mind stands in the way. You know why that is? It's because others have said you were bad and they made you live in bad conditions. When a man hears that over and over and looks about him and sees that his life is bad, he begins to doubt his own mind. His feelings drag him forward and his mind, full of what others say about him, tells him to go back. The job in getting people to fight and have faith is in making them believe in what life has made them feel, making them feel that their feelings are as good as those of others.

'Bigger, the people who hate you feel just as you feel, only they're on the other side of the fence. You're black, but that's only a part of it. Your being black, as I told you before, makes it easy for them to single you out. Why do they do that? They want the things of life, just as you did, and they're not particular about how they get them. They hire people and they don't pay them enough; they take what people own and build up power. They rule and regulate life. They have things arranged so that they can do those things and the people can't fight back. They do that to black people more than others because they say that black people are inferior. But, Bigger, they say that *all* people who work are inferior. And the rich people don't want to change things; they'll lose too much. But deep down in them they feel like you feel, Bigger, and in order to keep what they've got, they make themselves believe that men who work are not quite human. They do like you did,

Bigger, when you refused to feel sorry for Mary. But on both sides men want to live; men are fighting for life. Who will win? Well, the side that feels life most, the side with the most humanity and the most men. That's why . . . y-you've got to b-believe in yourself, Bigger . . .'

Max's head jerked up in surprise when Bigger laughed.

'Ah, I reckon I believe in myself . . . I ain't got nothing else . . . I got to die . . .'

He stepped over to Max. Max was leaning against the window.

'Mr Max, you go home. I'm all right . . . Sounds funny, Mr Max, but when I think about what you say I kind of feel what I wanted. It makes me feel I was kind of right . . .' Max opened his mouth to say something and Bigger drowned out his voice. 'I ain't trying to forgive nobody and I ain't asking for nobody to forgive me. I ain't going to cry. They wouldn't let me live and I killed. Maybe it ain't fair to kill, and I reckon I really didn't want to kill. But when I think of why all the killing was, I begin to feel what I wanted, what I am . . .'

Bigger saw Max back away from him with compressed lips. But he felt he had to make Max understand how he saw things now.

'I didn't want to kill!' Bigger shouted. 'But what I killed for, I *am*! It must've been pretty deep in me to make me kill! I must have felt it awful hard to murder . . .'

Max lifted his hand to touch Bigger, but did not.

'No; no; no . . . Bigger, not that . . .' Max pleaded despairingly.

'What I killed for must've been good!' Bigger's voice was full of frenzied anguish. 'It must have been good! When a man kills, it's for something . . . I didn't know I was really alive in this world until I felt things hard enough to kill for 'em . . . It's the truth, Mr Max. I can say it now, 'cause I'm going to die. I know what I'm saying real good and I know how it sounds. But I'm all right. I feel all right when I look at it that way . . .'

Max's eyes were full of terror. Several times his body moved nervously, as though he were about to go to Bigger; but he stood still.

'I'm all right, Mr Max. Just go and tell Ma I was all right and not to worry none, see? Tell her I was all right and wasn't crying none . . .'

Max's eyes were wet. Slowly, he extended his hand. Bigger shook it.

'Good-bye, Bigger,' he said quietly.

'Good-bye, Mr Max.'

Max groped for his hat like a blind man; he found it and jammed it on his head. He felt for the door, keeping his face averted. He poked his arm through and signaled for the guard. When he was let out he stood for a moment, his back to the steel door. Bigger grasped the bars with both hands.

'Mr Max . . .'

'Yes, Bigger.' He did not turn around.

'I'm all right. For real, I am.'

'Good-bye, Bigger.'

'Good-bye, Mr Max.'

Max walked down the corridor.

'Mr Max!'

Max paused, but did not look.

'Tell . . . Tell Mister . . . Tell Jan hello . . .'

'All right, Bigger.'

'Good-bye!'

'Good-bye!'

He still held on to the bars. Then he smiled a faint, wry, bitter smile. He heard the ring of steel against steel as a far door clanged shut.

© Hulton Archive / Getty Images

RICHARD WRIGHT was born in Mississippi in 1908. As a child he lived in Memphis, Tennessee, then in an orphanage, and with various relatives – each proved painful, yet formative experiences which he eventually wrote about in his autobiography, *Black Boy*. Wright left home at fifteen and in 1934 went to Chicago, where in 1935 he began to work on the Federal Writers' Project. His first book, *Uncle Tom's Children*, a collection of novellas, was published in 1938 and Wright was awarded a Guggenheim Fellowship in the following year.

Wright went on to write many more essay collections, non-fiction books and novels, including *The Outsider* and *Native Son*, of which parts are extracted here. Through his writing, Wright confronted the issues of race relations and the plight of African Americans head on. Because of this his work has often been marked by controversy and impassioned criticism, even from otherwise supportive contemporaries, such as James Baldwin, who took particular exception to the character of Bigger Thomas.

After the Second World War, Richard Wright went to live in Paris with his wife and daughters, remaining there until his death in 1960.

RECOMMENDED BOOKS BY RICHARD WRIGHT:

*Black Boy*
*Native Son*

# How do we combat Injustice?

Love
JEANETTE WINTERSON

VINTAGE MINIS

Friendship
ROSE TREMAIN

VINTAGE MINIS

Language
XIAOLU GUO

VINTAGE MINIS

Freedom
MARGARET ATWOOD

VINTAGE MINIS

## VINTAGE MINIS

The Vintage Minis bring you some of the world's greatest writers on the experiences that make us human. These stylish, entertaining little books explore the whole spectrum of life – from birth to death, and everything in between. Which means there's something here for everyone, whatever your story.

vintageminis.co.uk